P

The Lightning Tree

"Captivating. With lyrical prose and an engrossing combination of supernatural mystery and slow-burn romance, *The Lightning Tree* takes readers on an emotional journey as Flora Reed's dedication to her sister leads to a most unlikely discovery about her family's traumatic past and the future of the planet. An excellent addition to the Cli-Fi genre, fans of Jim Lynch's *The Highest Tide* and Francesca Lia Block's *Love in the Time of Global Warming* will connect to this cautionary tale."

—Amalie Jahn, author of *Phoebe Unfired* and *The Next to Last Mistake*

"*The Lightning Tree* is unlike anything I've ever read, which is rare in YA. It is an environmental thriller interlaced with tragically separated sisters, burgeoning romance, and elements of true horror. Lene Fogelberg is a refreshing new voice and I can't wait to see where the series goes next!"

—Carolyn Cohagan, author of The Time Zero Trilogy

"We are at a tipping point in history, a potential extinction event, and must heed that fact or accept the consequences. In *The Lightning Tree*, Fogelberg distills this message into a timely and important novel that compels the reader to confront a broken relationship with nature."

—David Massey, award-winning author of *Torn* and *Taken*

THE

LIGHTNING

TREE

THE

LIGHTNING

TREE

BOOK I,
THE NATURAL INTELLIGENCE
REVOLUTION TRILOGY

A Novel

LENE FOGELBERG

DEDAUN
PUBLISHING

Published 2022
Dedaun Publishing
dedaun.publishing@gmail.com

Printed in the United States of America
ISBN: 978-91-987476-0-7 pbk
ISBN: 978-91-987476-1-4 ebk

Cover design by Andrew Davis
Book design by Stacey Aaronson

This is a work of fiction. Names, characters, places, and incidents either are the product of the author's imagination or are used fictitiously. Any resemblance to actual persons, living or dead, is entirely coincidental.

"The earth laughs in flowers."

—RALPH WALDO EMERSON

I

FLORA

ME AND FAUNA.

Always me and Fauna.

I remember every moment of that day.

Her searching for me in the tall grass, calling out "Flora?" *Flora . . . Flora . . .* My name ringing under the bluebell sky.

The memory is etched in my mind, along with the lightning marks on my skin: pink zigzags across my neck, my chest, my arms, like the branches of the tree where it happened. Like the flash of lightning that changed everything.

I remember the green caterpillar measuring the edge of my sketchbook, the paper patterned by sunlight and mud stains. The half-drawn bluebells on the page all shaky from me drawing the lines again and again, the side of my hand graphite gray. My ribs pressing against the ground, the dry grass tickling my bare legs.

Flora . . . Flora . . . Flora . . .

And then I hear a distant rumble, a flock of crows cawing,

Fauna shouting from the oak tree, her clear voice asking, "Where are you?"

I look up and the sky has turned an angry purple, breathing chilly gusts down my neck. From afar, I can see Fauna's ginger hair like a single fall leaf in the vibrant green.

"Fauna! No!" Forgetting bluebells and sketchbook, I dash through the meadow, buzzing insects fleeing like sparks around me. Another rumble, louder now, and the sky opens into an instant downpour. I run faster, my cotton skirt sticking to my thighs.

When I reach the oak tree, I pull a wet strand of hair from my eyes. "Fauna." Her name tastes like rain. "Come down."

"Oh, there you are," she says, reaching for another branch. My butterfly of a little sister: three years younger than my sixteen, she's a flurry of sharp knees and elbows, of freckles and bronze curls.

The sky rumbles again as I pull myself up the trunk, my hands and feet finding the pockets in the oak's limbs that I used to know as well as Fauna. She's sitting out on a branch, too far out.

"Fauna," I gasp. "You need to come down."

She shakes her head. "Dad's not here." She pulls herself up and sways unsteadily, one hand clutching the branch above her. "He can't tell us what to do anymore."

I cling to the trunk, the bark rough under my fingers. "No, I mean, because of the thunder and—"

She interrupts me. "Remember how he used to freak out

when we climbed up here?" She pulls her chin to her chest, her voice deepening. "You know you're not allowed in the oak tree!" And then she sinks down, bending over to hug the branch. "I don't remember much of him, but I remember that."

I follow her gaze to the empty graveled driveway where, had he been here, our father would have been standing, yelling at us. The rain hums its steady melody, pattering against the leaves, but here, under the dense canopy of the tree, it's as though we're sitting in a leafy cave with only a gentle drizzle dripping through.

"There was this song you used to sing up here," I say. Maybe if I can make her think of something besides our absent father, I might be able to make her come down. "Something about a blue jay."

Pulling herself up, Fauna lets out her hiccup laughter and starts to sing. "Two blue jays sat in a tree. One was stung by a beeeee." Flinging back her head, she stretches the note into a high-pitched arc, and I have to smile, recognizing her made-up song from when we were little. "And one had to flee. No more blue jays sat in the treeee."

Another rumble, and I hug the oak's trunk tighter, inhaling the earthy scent of moss, searching for something, anything, to make Fauna come down. Through the leaves, I glimpse the weathered siding of our old farmhouse, the billowing grass in the meadow, the tilted shed overgrown by vines in our backyard. Around it all, the wall of trees stands shoulder to shoulder like silent guards watching the entrance to the woods.

Fauna has stopped singing. Now she's sitting on the branch again, legs swinging. She turns to me. "You'll leave me too, eventually. You'll go off to college." Her forget-me-not blue eyes widen. "You'll disappear, just like Dad."

I let out a chuckle, shaking my head. "I will never leave you." Another rumble rolls over us, closer this time. "Never," I repeat, feeling raindrops dripping on my scalp and running down my spine under my t-shirt, making me shiver. I spot twin acorns at the end of a twig right next to me and pick them, leaves and all. "We're like this." I hold out the acorns. "You and me."

Fauna grabs the branch above her and pulls herself up, balancing toward me, her t-shirt and cut-off jeans wet in uneven blotches, clinging to her skinny body.

"Yeah?" She stretches out her hand. "Can I see?"

My fingers brush briefly against hers, but then she turns and starts humming that song again, her words as free and ever-changing as she is.

"Two acorns sat in a tree . . ."

A surge of cold air rustles through the leaves and there's another rumble over the treetops, the sky growling like an animal.

"Fauna," I plead. "Come down."

She's still singing, twirling the twig with the acorns. "One was—"

And then, a sword of light cuts the world in half. I reach for her, but she is already falling. My Fauna, my little sister, her wide, forget-me-not eyes, her hand still holding the acorns, her head *thump, thump, thumping* from branch to branch to ground.

Everything roars: the sky, the meadow, the trunk in my arms. My hands, my chest, my bones burn. I can't breathe. I can't move. I can't even scream. I'm paralyzed by the current moving through me until suddenly, I force the air down in one gasp and then another.

But Fauna is lying completely still. She's cradled by the roots of the tree, her white t-shirt burning at the edges. My whole body in pain, I haul myself down, down, down to the muddy ground.

"Noooooooo!" I sob.

I grab her hand but her fingers are stiff, her gaze fixed on the purple sky, rain filling her eyes. The smell of burnt grass engulfs me as I lower my ear to her chest. I feel Fauna's sharp ribs, her rain-soaked t-shirt against my cheek. In the trunk of the tree, a glowing wound traces the jagged line where she fell.

Blinking rain and tears, I see a shadow approaching. It's Mom running toward us—bare feet, tangled copper hair, screaming with no words, enfolding me in an empty, hollow sound.

2

Fauna

One second I am thirteen, the next I am a hundred years old.

I can feel the years branching out into my bones, the wind blowing through me, the ground reaching for me, opening itself up and swallowing me.

I can feel the lightning running through me, charging the ground, the grass, burning my fingertips, my leaves, my feet, my roots.

But all I can think about is my sister—clinging to me, her fingers digging into my skin, the rain falling in torrents over us. I mustn't drop her.

I mustn't drop her.

3

FLORA

One Year Later

TAP-TAP.

That sound. Like a stubborn bird pecking my window. I pull the pillow over my head.

Tap-tap-tap.

"Okay, okay." I drag myself out of bed and peer out the window, squinting in the bright light. There he is, standing in our yard, arm raised and ready to fire again. I lift the sash and the whole summer morning explodes into my room: birds chirping, pungent whiffs of cut grass—and sharp pieces of gravel hitting my face.

"Ouch!" I stick my head out. "I'm awake! I'm awake!"

"Sorry." Carl chuckles, those dimples like punctuation marks completing his smile in both directions. "Sleepyhead."

He's carrying his black military-style backpack, up early and ready to absorb knowledge like the prodigy he is, even though it's the last day before summer break.

"I wasn't sleeping," I say. But I'm still squinting.

"Yeah, right." He chuckles again.

I sigh and rub my eyes. "Why didn't you text me, like a normal person?"

"Your phone's off."

"Oh." I reach toward my desk. "I forgot to charge it." I find the cord nestled between the wide wooden floorboards and plug the phone in.

"You coming?" His question ends with the *thud* of his backpack against the porch.

"Just give me a sec." I find my favorite pair of cut-offs folded in the laundry basket on the floor and change from my old sleeping t-shirt into an even older t-shirt, one of Fauna's—the black one with white dots sprinkled all over it, like a starry night sky. It's way too small, but I don't mind. It reminds me of the Fauna who was more than what happened to her: Fauna the stargazer, Fauna the singer of crazy made-up songs, Fauna the tree climber.

I stop by the mirror on the wall next to my desk and see my whole room inverted in the glass: my wrought-iron bed with the wrinkled sheets, my floral walls covered in roses, the open window with the white cotton curtains blowing in the breeze.

And then the light catches the glimmering silver *F* dangling from a chain around my neck. We each got one from Mom shortly before the accident. The gifts were a surprise one day, just because "you're the best kiddos ever."

"You coming, or what?" Carl's voice echoes from the

yard and I realize I've been in a daze, tracing the faded marks engraved on my neck and chest and arms, branching out like pink flashes of lightning.

"I'm coming!" I grab my phone from my desk, barely charged, and stuff it into my canvas shoulder bag. On my way down the stairs, I pull my unruly blond hair into a ponytail, but it still reaches my waist.

Mom raises her head from *The Pennsylvania Gazette* as I fly into the kitchen. Her red curls glow in the sunlight seeping through the lace curtains, painting the whole room in a golden hue. For a second, her gaze drifts to a spot next to me, and I know she is looking at the emptiness I constantly carry beside me: the girl who should have been here.

"Last day, huh?" Mom's hands cling tightly to her mug of tea, like she's freezing all the way to her bones, despite the warm morning. "Wasn't I supposed to sign a report card or some—"

I interrupt her with a hug from behind, wrapping my arms around her as if I could melt the cold away. "Don't worry about it, I'll show you later."

"Yeah, I guess it's all online these days," she sighs. Her shoulders sink and she fumbles to take my hand. "Are you going to see her today?"

I nod into her copper hair, a couple of strands tickling my chin. "After school."

Mom turns to look at me, her pale blue eyes reminding me of Fauna's. "I'll try to come too." There's a trace of a smile, of the Mom I used to know, and I give her a tight squeeze.

She shakes me off and chuckles, straightening her denim shirt. "Now get out of here, kiddos!"

We both hear it, the last syllable that came out of habit, and Mom's smile is gone in an instant.

"Carl's waiting for me," I say awkwardly.

She nods.

I find Carl on the porch swing. "That didn't take long," he says. In one leap, he grabs his backpack and follows me down the steps to the driveway. His sarcasm usually makes me laugh, but my chest feels tight, like laughter would suffocate me.

"You okay, flower-girl?" He bumps into my side on purpose, and that small jolt loosens the knot in my chest.

"Yeah, sure." I bump him back, and we break into a run. We pass under the oak tree, the gravel crackling below our feet, as the memory cuts through me like the bolt of lightning on that terrible day, the *thump, thump, thump* of Fauna's head from branch to branch to ground. My skin burns, as if my body remembers the pain.

Once we're out of the tree's shadow, I exhale slowly and the burning subsides.

"Wait till you hear this—" Carl says. He kicks the gravel, sending a swarm of pebbles into the street as we come around the hawthorn hedge onto Pine Ridge Road.

"What?"

Far down the street we see the back of the yellow school bus disappear around the corner to Maple Street. "Oh, man!" Carl says. "We missed it."

I spill a sharp piece of gravel out of my shoe, jumping on one foot. "I guess we'll have to walk." I wobble and reach for Carl's broad shoulder. He lends himself to support me, his arms crossed over his chest.

"You done?" he says. His brown eyes have that softness in them that sends a tingle down my spine.

I nod and let go of his shoulder. We continue down the sloping road, passing the brick colonial where Carl is living with the Owens, his foster parents of almost a year.

"What did you start to tell me?" I ask.

"Oh right." Carl rolls his eyes. "I got grounded last night for being ten minutes late, can you believe it?" He turns to me and snorts. "It's not like I'm doing drugs or anything."

"That sucks," I say.

I have to constantly remind myself that things like getting grounded and missing the bus are normal teenage things—and I have to give normal a try, even though nothing is the way it used to be. At least Carl understands better than anyone about voids that follow you wherever you go. We both have nothing but vague memories of our dads, and his mom has been dead for years. She was ripped out of his life suddenly too. Lightning strike, car accident, it all hurts the same when you're one of the people left behind. I didn't think I'd meet someone who'd understand about Fauna, and then suddenly he showed up, living next door, walking with me to school, calling me *flower-girl.*

"Come on," Carl says, speeding up, his sneakers beating the asphalt. He's one step ahead of me and I swoon a bit over his beautiful brown skin, his gray t-shirt that crawls up under his backpack, his washed-out jeans, his wide shoulders slightly jutted forward like he's constantly ready to take off.

Across the street, Mrs. Walsh, still in her pink bathrobe and hair curlers, picks up her newspaper and gives us a nod before closing the door to her rose-covered cottage.

Carl slows down and gently elbows me. "Are you coming to the party tonight?"

I stop and throw a hand on my hip. With a playful squint, I say, "Carl Nielsen, don't try to lure me to one of your crazy all-nighters."

The two sides of Carl are a mystery that I can't quite reconcile: the math genius and the friends-with-everybody party animal.

"Flora Reed, one party's not going to kill you," he says.

I realize I can't joke my way out of this and take a deep breath. "I'm not going."

"Come on," Carl teases, "you need to get out more, not stay in your room like a whopping hermit." He says *whopping*, his new favorite word, like a whiplash.

"Just drop it, will you?" I turn away from him, like I'm suddenly interested in the front yard we're passing, full of brightly colored toys and bicycles.

"No, I will not drop it because I want you to come to this party with me." His voice is unusually serious. "You're allowed to have fun, you know."

My eyelids are burning, but I'm not going to cry. "I thought you were grounded," I mumble.

He turns to walk backward in front of me, flashing me that dimpled smile of his. "Nothing can stop me, flower-girl."

"Don't call me that." I reach out to give him a push, but he leaps away and circles back beside me again, giving me another side bump that shoves me into the bushes.

"Hey!" I wail. I pull myself out of the mass of twigs and leaves, ready to smack his head, but he is already dashing down the street.

"If I get there first," he calls out, "you have to come to the party!"

I have no choice but to run for it. I turn off the street and follow him down the narrow lane between houses, over the small bridge across the silver ribbon of Pine Creek that shimmers between the trees. I almost overtake him on the grassy trail behind a row of backyards, but then he beats me up the hill and comes to a halt, bouncing on his toes by the football field.

When I reach him, he is already doing his victory dance, running around in circles, arms over his head, shouting "Paaar-tay!"

I lean over to catch my breath. The lightning marks on the back of my hands and arms are tingling, but I can't help laughing. Now Carl's turning his back to me, doing the robot dance. "Par-ty, par-ty, par-ty," he chants.

This is my chance.

"So long, sucker!" I say. I dash across the football field toward the cluster of low brick buildings, not caring about the mud squirting up my legs, or the ponytail coming loose so my hair flaps against my back.

Behind me, Carl is shouting, "You still need to come, flower—" but I have already reached the back door. Breathless, I pull it open and stumble into the mess of euphoric kids and end-of-year banners and slamming lockers that is the corridor of Derwyn High School.

4

FAUNA

I sense you running past me, and you're like water through my fingers, impossible to grasp, always out of reach.

No matter how I stretch, farther and farther, it is never enough.

I'm so close to your bedroom window. A few yards, that's all it would take for me to tap the glass.

I am here.

I am here.

5

FLORA

MR. SLOANE COMES THROUGH THE DOOR OF SCIENCE class, balancing yearbooks in a pile against his chest, his brown tie caught between the books. With a *wham*, he drops the yearbooks on his desk and straightens to gaze around the classroom, scratching his chin.

I shrink, wrapping my feet around the legs of my chair, but he spots me and lets out a deep sigh. "Miss Reed, I believe you are the only one who has yet to deliver their presentation." He pats the stack on his desk. "You can all have your yearbooks afterward."

A murmur erupts from the class and someone coughs a "C'mon."

My hands are suddenly clammy against the desktop. On the scratched surface, someone has scribbled *THE END IS NEAR* with a black marker.

Mr. Sloane continues, "It's the last day. No way to postpone." He pronounces every syllable carefully, like the words are ingredients in a lab experiment, meticulously measured.

No more excuses.

I bring my laptop and notebook to the front of the classroom, my knees trembling. I avoid looking at the class as I fumble with the cords. My fingers don't seem like my own anymore as I awkwardly plug the projector cord into my laptop.

I stand back and brush a strand of hair from my face. My heartbeat is a rising rhythm in my ears.

The murmur in the classroom settles into a low hum of whisperings. A chair scrapes against the floor. A foot taps against the leg of a table.

"Um," I say, searching for the right words. I have rehearsed so many times in front of the mirror, and still my mind is completely blank. "So, climate change," I start, and flip through the pages in my notebook.

"What?" a guy in the back shouts. I look up and see Jack Dunne in his blue-and-white varsity jacket, a smirk on his face.

Mr. Sloane clears his throat. "Miss Reed, you need to speak up."

I take a deep breath and click to the first slide in my presentation, a picture of a verdant rain forest. The notebook is shaking in my hands, and the words seem to crawl away across the pages. "The well-being of the Earth's forests and our climate are inseparably linked together."

I click to the next picture, a wasteland with stubs instead of trees. "Deforestation is one of the biggest contributors to greenhouse gas and climate change." I pause and look up, but everything is melting into a blur—the students at their desks, the glass cabinets along the walls, the row of sinks in the back, Mr. Sloane sitting on a chair by the door. I look down again and focus on the squiggly letters in my notebook.

"These ecosystems are often called the lungs of the world since they turn carbon dioxide into oxygen. Without forests, we would die."

I click to the next picture, a football field. "Still, the deforestation is so severe that we're losing forests at a rate of thirty football fields per minute. It's like we're slowly choking ourselves."

Mr. Sloane interrupts me. "Miss Reed, you need to stop mumbling."

I feel my cheeks burn, the blush spreading across my face to my hairline. I force a smile and struggle to raise my voice. "More than eighty percent of deforestation happens in just eleven places."

Crap. I forgot to change pictures. I click to the map I prepared, with the danger zones marked in red.

"As we can see on this map . . ." I feel the lightning marks on my neck burn and pulsate. "As we can see . . ."

The girls in the middle row are whispering and giggling.

"As we can . . ." I turn to the next page in my notebook,

but it's all a blur now. I wish Carl were here to send me one of his dimpled smiles that says, *You've got this, flower-girl.* My heart is pounding harder and I feel like my knees will give out.

"Thank you," I mumble, and close my laptop.

On my way to my seat, I drop the notebook on the floor. When I bend to pick it up, the silence is worse than the whispering and the giggles. Swallowing the tears, I sit down in my chair. I didn't give even half of my presentation. I had meant to end with, "We all need to come together to fight deforestation and climate change." My heart is still pounding in my ears. *Failure, failure, failure.*

WHEN CLASS ENDS, Mr. Sloane motions for me to stay behind.

"Remember to breathe," he says, "and you'll do better next time." He sits on his desk and smooths his brown tie over his pale yellow shirt. "I know you have a lot on your mind."

My heart sinks. "I'm sorry . . ." Searching for something to say, I shift the yearbook and laptop in my arms, the metal cold against my skin.

Mr. Sloane stands up and grabs his briefcase. "I'll give you a D." Before I can say anything, he adds, "Take care, Miss Reed." His eyes linger on my arms for a moment, on my faded lightning marks, and I realize he just bumped my grade from an F.

Because I am *that girl.*

I swallow hard and nod, then join the hordes of juniors on their way to their lockers in the hall.

AFTER SPENDING SPANISH class watching *La Bella Durmiente*, half asleep with my head in my arms on the desk, and then an hour with the rest of eleventh grade listening to Vice Principal Harrison in the auditorium ("Don't drink and drive, kids, we want to see all of you back here in the fall."), I am finally free.

My yearbook pressed to my chest, I zigzag down the mobbed corridor, pushing between the crowds of elated students and relieved teachers.

I open my yearbook to see what the girls in my Spanish class wrote. *Have a great summer! You're the best! Abrazos y besos XOXO.*

My shoulders drop. I don't know what I was hoping for. I'm used to this by now, the invisible wall between me and most people—how they are nice but keep their distance, like I am bad luck. Be with me and get struck by lightning. Be with me and fall out of a tree.

But then there's Carl. He hollered "Paaar-tay!" every time he passed me in the corridor today, and now, he bumps into me with his wide smile and dimples.

"Hey, flower-girl, I've been looking for you."

I love how we don't even have to say anything. We just exchange yearbooks on our way through the doors, following the current of students down the stairs to freedom. All the way, Carl gives out fist bumps and high-fives. I have lived in this town for most of my life, yet he seems more at home after less than a year than I do. And he treats everyone the same: nerds, jocks, girls, even teachers. Like it doesn't matter to him what anyone would think or say about him.

When we reach the edge of the parking lot, we climb onto our bench under the birch trees, sitting on the backrest with our feet on the seat. Carl digs out a pen from his backpack and I snatch it from him.

"Thanks," I smirk.

"Hey!" he protests, digging out another one.

I flip through his yearbook. Every page is full of scribbles except the last one. I glance up him as he bends over my yearbook, his thumb beating a quiet rhythm against the page. My lightning marks tingle again, but I ignore it. A gentle breeze blows through the birches as I begin to write. It's a blue ballpoint pen with perfect flow and I can't resist doodling in all directions, flowers stretching their leaves toward the center of the page where I draw our neighboring houses, bees buzzing between them. I'm careful with the details—the bricks in the Owens' house, the porch and lace kitchen curtains on mine. I even draw Carl and me sitting in our bedroom windows. Above it all, I write in my best handwriting:

Have fun with the math wizards.
~~Love,~~ See you around, Flora

I draw a flock of birds to cover *Love*. I don't know what I was thinking writing that. Fortunately, he's not going anywhere, since the math summer camp he's volunteering at is right here in Derwyn.

"You writing an essay?" Carl teases, trying to grab his yearbook from me as I turn away.

"Wait," I insist. I need to fill in the birds so the letters don't bleed through. "Okay, done." I close the book and hand it back.

Carl immediately flips it open to the last page. "Whoa."

He studies my drawing, which covers the entire page. His eyes widen as his mouth falls open. "You're really good."

"Yeah?" I say. I had forgotten this feeling, the magic of filling an empty space simply by moving a pen or a brush over it. "You like it?"

"Like it?" Carl is still staring at my drawing. "You're a whopping genius!"

I smile and snatch my yearbook from his lap. I want to read what he wrote to me but don't know if I should, not while he's sitting there. If it's another *You're the best!* I might not be able to hide my disappointment.

"Why don't you draw like this anymore?" Carl asks. He bites his lip, like he's already regretting the words.

I feel my eyes burning. *Why does he always make me feel like I'm going to cry?* I get up from the bench, blinking away the tears.

I don't answer his question. Instead, I just say, "Thanks," then wave my yearbook and add, "See you later."

He gives me a nod with that wide smile of his before I turn to cross the steaming hot parking lot.

"See you tonight," I hear Carl shout. "At the paaar-tay!"

6

FAUNA

The vast blue, the shades of green, the dark earth, it's all here when I close my eyes.

Open, close.

Here, here, all the time.

Until it isn't.

7

FLORA

IT'S JUST A SHORT WALK ACROSS TOWN TO WHITE
Oak Manor. Fortunately, I cleaned out my locker yesterday,
and I only have to carry my yearbook. I could put it in my
shoulder bag along with my laptop and notebook, but I like
the way it feels in my hands. Any moment I could flip it open
to see what Carl wrote. But I don't. Not yet.

It's a beautiful day. I wish Fauna were here with me,
walking down Main Street like we used to, her skipping and
bouncing beside me on our way to the Book Nook. Mom
would look over and smile, hearing the doorbell announce
us coming through the door. "Did you have a good day, kiddos?" she'd always ask.

I stop in front of the shop window and can nearly see
Fauna's reflection next to mine—her pale face and her wild
ginger hair—but it's a ghost, a memory, a wish.

Over my head hangs the wooden sign in the shape of an
open book. Ornate, emerald letters scroll across the weath-

ered boards: THE WEE REED BOOK NOOK. I remember Mom's sweeping arms as we painted the sign years ago, her voice trembling with excitement. *Bring books to the people! Shelves full of stories! A meeting place for bookworms of all ages!* That was when we were still little, before Dad left. Before Fauna's accident.

I can see her now by the counter, talking to a bent, gray-haired lady. Mom is holding up a book, calmly turning a page, nodding. I miss her grand gestures, her loud laughter.

Suddenly Mom looks up and sees me. She breaks into a smile. I wave and smile back. She blows me a kiss and then her eyes wander to the empty spot beside me. I don't think she's aware that she does that.

Sometimes I feel like she blames me, like I can hear words in my head she has never said. *You should have taken better care of your little sister. You shouldn't have let her fall.* In a way, it would be a relief if she would just say it out loud, instead of with her wandering eyes and strained smiles.

The hunched lady at the counter drops her purse and Mom hurries to help her. I turn to continue down Main Street, the shadows of the linden trees painting stripes over the sidewalk. A red convertible drives past, full of screaming seniors with their arms in the air.

I don't mind walking; not needing to drive everywhere is one of the benefits of living in a small town, which is good because Mom is trying to cut back on expenses. It's balmy today, though, and the heat makes the yearbook stick to my

hands as I cross the town square. Carl's message is still waiting in the back of the book like a gift I barely dare to open.

I pass through the shadow cast by the two-hundred-
year-old white oak that takes up the center of the square.
The sudden coolness here always makes me shiver. Walking
in the flickering pattern of light and shadow and gazing up
into the thick branches, I wonder what the tree has witnessed. The Welsh immigrants who cleared the forest and
settled our small town? The raising of Derwyn Town Hall,
its tall spire like an arrow pointing to the sky behind the
oak's crown? The row of shops popping up on Main Street
and the streets branching out, farther and farther? The con-
struction of the stately White Oak Manor and the lives of
the family living there, decade after decade, until it was
turned into an assisted living home?

My lightning marks are tingling again, as if there's some
sort of language whispered in my skin, pulsating, billowing,
like the leaves in the breeze above me. No, I have to push
away these crazy thoughts; the stinging is just damaged
nerves in my scarred skin, nothing more.

Rubbing my arm, I cut across the well-tended lawn, the
grass tickling my ankles. I amble up the paved walkway that
leads up to the colonial two-story façade of white pillars and
black shutters. I shove the heavy door open and there is
Rhonda at the reception, beaming at me.

"I knew you were coming," she says with a smile. "Last
day of school and everything."

I smile back. "Hi Rhonda."

Ms. Mayfair sits in the parlor in her floral dress and I wave at her as a reflex, then let my hand sink, remembering she's blind as her dim eyes stare off into the distance.

"Hi, Ms. Mayfair," I call out.

She flinches and smiles. "Hello sweetie. Such a beautiful day." She waves as I walk past, then I head down the hall until I reach the room at the end.

The door is open a crack. Bright sunlight seeps out into the hallway and touches the toes of my sneakers. I knock softly before entering.

Fauna sits by the window, her ginger hair glowing, facing the garden in her wheelchair. I hesitate. Maybe she's sleeping? I'll never get used to how thin she is; her knees sharp under her gray sweatpants make her look younger than the fourteen-year-old she is.

I hear footsteps behind me, and then the cheery voice of Abigail, one of Fauna's nurses. "That's her favorite place to sit."

I turn to her and nod. "Looking out to the sky."

Abigail's bright eyes wander between me and Fauna as she shakes her head, her graying blond hair brushing against her shoulders. "I came to start the physiotherapy." She leans in close, putting a warm hand on my arm. A whiff of bleach rises from her white scrubs. "But it can wait a while, dear."

"Thanks," I say. "I appreciate it." I pull up a chair and sit next to Fauna.

"Just holler if you need me." Abigail says, leaving a gap in the door so I can hear her puttering in the hallway.

"Hi, Fauna," I say. I search her pale face for a reaction, something to tell me she recognizes my voice. Her forget-me-not blue eyes are resting on the maple tree in the garden, but I can't tell if she's actually looking at it. Her gaze seems to have that special softness it gets when resting on nature. It pains me to see her like this. She used to be a chatterbox, never running out of things to say. I used to be the quiet one.

"Today was the last day of school," I tell her. I pull a shimmering strand of hair from her cheek. "Nothing much happened, we pretty much just watched movies."

I don't want to tell her about my catastrophic science presentation, so I look around the room instead—at the neatly made hospital bed, the pink geraniums on top of the chest of drawers, the wall covered with photos and get-well cards from back when people thought she would get better. Some of them hang crookedly, the tape starting to come loose. She doesn't get cards anymore and it's been a long time since she got visits from her friends.

"We had to sit in the auditorium for an hour," I say. "You would have hated it." I have the yearbook in my lap, my index finger tracing the embossed block letters spelling out DERWYN HIGH SCHOOL.

Unable to wait any longer, I flip it open and search through the last pages until I see it.

HAVE A WHOPPING SUMMER, FLOWER-GIRL!
DON'T GET LOST IN THE BOOK NOOK. AND
CHARGE YOUR PHONE, SLEEPYHEAD.
YOUR DEVOTED ALARM CLOCK, CARL.

That boy, he's nearly made me cry again. It is perfect, the words are perfect, the drawing of a smiley-faced clock with stick arms and legs next to his name—it's all perfect.

I look up at Fauna. "There's this end-of-year party tonight." I sigh and reach for her hand. It's dry and warm, but there's no movement to indicate if she can feel my touch. "I'd rather stay here with you, but Carl is totally set on me coming." I follow her gaze to the garden and squeeze her hand. "So, I guess I'm going."

Slowly—so slowly I almost can't believe it's happening—Fauna turns her head and looks directly at me. I hold my breath; she has never done this before, not once in the year since the accident. I don't dare move or say anything. I just let the wide-open blue sky of her eyes envelop me. She begins to utter the letter *n* over and over, like she wants to say something. "N-n-n-n-n-n-n-n—"

"What is it, Fauna?" I nod, like I could draw words from her, but it's just the same stuttering, every *n* like an exhale.

"Noh-noh-noh-noh."

Her voice is different than how I remember it, deeper, urgent, like it hurts to speak.

I don't know what to do, what to say, and now she arches her back and starts to tremble all over, throwing her head from side to side against the neck rest on her wheelchair.

"Abigail!" I run to the door. "Abigail!" I can't see her anywhere. Where is she? "Something is wrong!" I call out.

Abigail comes running from someone's room. "What's happening, dear?"

"I don't know, I've never seen . . ."

We hurry back into Fauna's room and Abigail rushes to my sister, who's throwing herself back and forth and making the wheelchair wobble from side to side.

"She's having a seizure." Abigail cradles Fauna's face with her hands, holding tightly to keep her from banging her head. "Can you please press the alarm button?"

I press the red button on the control panel by Fauna's bed and a distant beeping goes off somewhere.

Abigail pulls the swaying wheelchair to the bed as Fauna continues stuttering, "Noh-noh-noh-noh."

Dr. Singh comes rushing through the door and then Rhonda, wheeling in a cart full of boxes and bottles. Everything happens so quickly. They lift Fauna to her bed, and I pull back, trying to stay out of the way. I watch them hold her down while Dr. Singh gives Abigail instructions on what injections and drugs to give. I feel helpless until I think of texting Mom. Maybe she'll be able to comfort Fauna, make her feel safe. I pull my phone from my pocket and there is just enough power to type a message.

Mom you better come Fauna
is having a seizure

Fauna is still throwing herself sideways and bending her legs like she's trying to run away lying down. *Please, Mom, check your phone.* I want to ask what's wrong with Fauna, but they seem too busy. Dr. Singh and Rhonda hold Fauna's hands and arms, while Abigail puts away the syringe.

Please, Mom, check your messages. My mouth tastes like blood; I realize I've been biting my lip. Suddenly I feel nauseous and fall back into the chair I'd pulled to the window. Was it only fifteen minutes ago? *Please, Mom, can you come?*

And then, Mom's voice echoes in the corridor. "I'm Ava Reed. I need to see my daughter." She rushes in, panting for air. She must have run all the way from the Book Nook. "What happened?" she asks.

Dr. Singh turns to Mom with a frown. "Mrs. Reed, your daughter had a seizure. We've given her a sedative and expect her to calm down promptly."

Mom gasps and dashes to Fauna's side. "My baby, what happened to you?" And then she spots me in the corner. "What did you do?" Her eyes are wild, I barely recognize her.

"I didn't—" I struggle to find the words. "I didn't do anything."

"You must have done something!" Mom shouts *something* like a curse word, like *something* might make you fall out of a tree.

"I just talked to her," I whisper, but Mom isn't listening. She's leaning over Fauna who's breathing calmly now, eyes closed, her head resting on the pillow.

Abigail takes me gently by the arm, pulling me to the door. "Come on, dear, there's nothing more we can do at the moment."

I pivot in the doorway. "Mom?"

She reaches into her purse. "Here," she snaps, holding out the keys to the Book Nook. "You might as well start your summer job today." Her voice is sharp, cutting the words at the edges.

I take the keys and glance over at Fauna, lying motionless in her bed, then follow Abigail down the corridor to reception. I barely listen to Abigail's reassurances. In my head, I can only hear, *What did you do? What did you do?*

"I don't know," I whisper. I open the heavy black door, trading the cool shade of White Oak Manor for the heat rising off the sidewalk. "I don't know."

8

FAUNA

No, no, no, no, no, no, no, no.

I can sense it, the undercurrent pulsating in my heart, in my burning veins.

The arrows of time pulling me closer, closer, no matter how I recoil, leaves trembling, roots resisting.

Like I am cut in two: half girl, half tree, half crown, half roots, sunshine and darkness all at once.

There's nothing I can do.

I can already sense the sharp axe, the smell of gasoline, the taste of blood.

9

FLORA

IT'S ALMOST SIX O'CLOCK.

I sigh, my arms resting against the worn wooden counter. The tingling in my skin is back, but so faint it's barely noticeable. I must be imagining it.

Hopefully Fauna is doing better. I check my phone for the hundredth time. No messages, but it's finally fully charged. I unplug it and let the cord fall to the floor. Turning it over and over, I make the phone do somersaults, bouncing against the counter, a stiff acrobat in a cherry blossom dress. Mom gave me the floral phone case, along with so many other flowery things—notebooks, bracelets, pencils—like offerings, as if I were an ancient Roman goddess. She once told me that Dad, ever the botanist, chose our names.

The phone against the wood is the only sound. *Clonk, clock, clonk.*

What did you do?

It's been a slow afternoon, the sole customer a thirty-something guy who browsed the poetry section for half an hour before deciding on T.S. Eliot's *The Waste Land*. My phone goes *ping*, and it's finally a message from Mom.

> Fauna is stable, still sleeping,
> but I need to stay and discuss
> her treatment with Abigail.
> Can you lock up?

Will do, I write back, and then I add:

> No problem

I cram my phone into my pocket and push the register open. We always lock the cash away in the antique safe that Mom found at a flea market in Philadelphia. I have been helping Mom for so long, I feel like I know every corner of this little shop, every shelf and rickety table propped up with books that lost their covers. I know every creaking step of the narrow stairs to the second floor, which is filled with more books—floor to ceiling—and the small kitchenette next to the old floral couch where we have instant noodles for lunch. There is only a tea-stained mug that reads *World's Best Mom* in the sink. Has she not eaten anything all day? I wash it and put it on the shelf next to our mismatched garage sale china.

Back downstairs I stop to inhale the musky, woody smell that I can trace all the way back to my childhood. Shimmering sunbeams find their way through the shop windows, throwing ribbons of sunlight across the floor-boards.

Sometimes I think Fauna is here, quietly running from bookcase to bookcase, playing hide and seek like when we were little, calling out from just around the corner of this shelf or that one, always out of reach, always *Come find me.* But it's just me.

I close the emerald front door and press my shoulder against its flaking paint so the key will turn. The afternoon is melting into evening, the shadows reaching for the row of shops across Main Street, but the golden air is still warm and sweet-smelling.

Ping. I pull out my phone. It's a message from Carl.

Where R U?

At the Book Nook, I answer. He texts back immediately.

U R coming, right?

I sigh and press the phone to my chest, leaning against the brick wall, rough against my elbows. The cars are passing by on Main Street, and a family carrying ice cream cones walks by me, the kids' faces all messy. The mom and dad are holding hands, and I smile. Mom and Dad used to hold hands too. Fauna and I used to have ice cream. We used to be a family like them.

I look down Main Street to the huge white oak tree by the town hall, its crown gilded by the sinking sun, and to the spot on the sidewalk where Mom would appear if she left White Oak Manor right now. Or now. Or now. But she doesn't come. I look down at the screen of my phone.

> OK, I'll just go home and
> change first, I text Carl.

He answers with three smiley faces, a party cracker, and a bunch of random animal emojis. I have to smile. Right, I am *such* a party animal.

I TUG AT my t-shirt, which barely reaches the waist of my denim skirt. My belly shows when I raise my arm to pull my hand through my hair, but I don't care. This was Fauna's favorite shirt, saying *I am here* in black cursive letters across my chest.

The cars are starting to line the street a block from the Dunnes', and I can hear the beat of the music even before I walk up the driveway of the modern architectural wonder that is the Dunnes' residence. The brightly lit floor-to-ceiling windows show the people inside, like an aquarium, and I stop for a moment to see if I can spot Carl, but there's no sign of him.

I wonder how Fauna is doing, if there's any change.

Mom wasn't back yet when I was leaving, so I left her a note on the kitchen table.

I'm at the end-of-year party at the Dunne's place. I won't be late.

Out on the porch, I ran back inside.

Don't worry, I added to the note, perhaps as much for my own sake as for Mom's.

I try to shake off thoughts of Mom and Fauna and turn into someone carefree, someone fun—a party cat or panda or chicken or whatever other animal Carl texted me.

As I start up the walkway, a dark-haired man and a blond woman step out of the house and wave at the guests inside. "Don't get any ideas, kids," the man shouts, "we'll be right next door." The woman laughs, and then we nearly stumble into each other.

"Oh, sorry," I mumble. "I'm Flora." I stretch out my hand.

"Hey, there." Mr. Dunne grabs my hand and squeezes it hard. "Don't make a mess of my house."

"She won't, silly." Mrs. Dunne slaps her husband's arm and sends me a smile, her eyes so narrow they're like happy cracks in her perfectly made-up face. "You won't, right?"

I'm just about to answer, but they have already strolled off. In their wake, a bunch of giggling sophomore girls stride past me. They don't ring the doorbell, just walk right in, and I follow them into the bright aquarium.

To the left is a large room where a couple of seniors are setting up for beer pong, but I don't see Carl anywhere. A group of kids files in behind me and I get pushed into a corner of the crowded hallway. I'm suddenly staring into a cabinet lit by spotlights. Inside is a row of hunting rifles, their polished muzzles pointing up to the ceiling. On the wall is a photograph of Mr. Dunne and his son, Jack, who's even taller than his dad, out on a hunting trip. Between them on the ground lies a large animal—a bear, a moose?

I need to get out of here. I squeeze myself between two laughing girls and head up the stairs.

It's less crowded on the second floor, but loud and hot. The rhythmic hip-hop music seems to pour from the ceiling, over kids lounging on a black leather sectional in the living room. The sun is setting, turning the tall, slightly opened windows into pink-orange-indigo impressionist paintings.

Leaning against the window frame, I inhale the cool air and exhale slowly. The view is breathtaking: I can see all over Derwyn—the spire of the town hall, the crown of the huge white oak tree. Somewhere in the dark shadows are White Oak Manor, Mom, and Fauna. Then the shadows move and change. It's the reflection in the glass of someone walking up to me.

"Hey, flower-girl, you came!"

And that's all it takes for a sudden warmth to spread through my chest. I twirl around and point to my t-shirt, smiling. *I am here.*

"Yes!" Carl pounds the air with his fist like he just won the grand prize at the Chester County Fair. "I knew I could lure you into coming." He chuckles and motions to the guy next to him. "You know Aaron, right? He's also volunteering at Math Wizards this summer."

Nodding, I take in Aaron's wavy brown hair, his wide smile. We have been orbiting around each other since middle school, in and out of the same classes, but have never really spoken to each other. "Hi, I'm Flora."

"Ouch." Aaron staggers back, his hand over his heart like I stabbed him. "You don't think I know your name?"

I laugh, and he seems to recuperate, imaginary dagger and all.

"But seriously," he adds, "it's crazy that we haven't hung out."

I don't know what to say, but Carl comes to the rescue.

"You want something to drink?" Then he hears how it sounds. "I mean, it's so whopping hot in here."

I laugh again, and before I can answer he says, "I'll get it for you." He turns and walks toward what must be the kitchen, and I have to suppress an urge to reach out for him and say *don't go.*

Now it's just me and Aaron, and even though the room is full of people talking, we seem to be standing in our own awkward bubble of silence.

"So, you—" Aaron shouts, but someone must have turned up the music because I can barely hear him. It's some sort of club dance music. I can feel the bass vibrate through the floor.

I shake my head at Aaron, and he motions for me to follow him. We push between people screaming to each other until we reach the kitchen, gleaming with marble and stainless steel. It's filled with people, but I don't see Carl.

Aaron pulls me to the island, where a bunch of guys are gathered around a mess of liquor bottles and beer cans. The center of attention is Jack Dunne, balancing a beer bottle on his chin. He is still wearing his varsity jacket, even though the kitchen is hot and stuffy. Next to him are Seth and Tyke, cheering him on as if he's about to score a touchdown.

"How about that?" Jack laughs and lets the bottle fall, catching it with one smooth movement. "Hey, Aaron, how's it going, man?" Jack grabs Aaron's hand and they bump shoulders the way boys do, and then Jack turns to me. "Hey, you're that girl—" He stops himself and lets the rest of the sentence hang between us, unspoken. But I know what he means: I am *that girl*.

His bloodshot gaze wanders up my arms to my neck.

"But really, what *are* those marks?"

I swallow. "Do you mean. . . ?" I hold out my scarred arms.

"Yes, your marks. What *is* that?" He grabs my arms and holds them up. I try to pull back, but his large hands have me locked like a bear trap.

I struggle to keep my voice cheerful. "They're called lightning trees, or lightning flowers." I wiggle to get free, but he doesn't let go. "Or Lichtenberg figures."

Jack squeezes my arms so hard it hurts, holding them to the light. "So, you really were struck by lightning." He studies the pale pattern of zigzags that crawl up my arms and disappear under my t-shirt.

"They used to be red, but they've faded," I offer, hoping he'll lose interest.

"Come on, man, let her go." Aaron puts a hand on Jack's shoulder, but Jack shrugs him off.

"Aren't they supposed to heal?" he asks.

"I don't know," I say. "I've never met anyone else who had them." *Except Fauna*, I think to myself. But I would never tell them about her lightning flower, the one on her chest right over her heart.

Seth reaches out to trace one of the marks along my forearm and shivers melodramatically. He then mimes a sleepwalker's face, tries to shove his beer into my hand, and says in a zombie voice, "Must. Share. Booze. Can't. Help. Giving. Witch. Beer." He shakes himself like he's waking up and says in his normal voice, "Some kind of magic."

Tyke leans in and starts to stroke my arm. The star-shaped silver ring on his middle finger presses against my scars. "This must be freaky unusual." He pushes his sticky fingers under the sleeve of my t-shirt. "Hey, they continue."

"Stop it!" I pull back, but he just laughs, letting his bulky ring follow the back of my arm as I shudder.

"Are you done?" Aaron wrestles Tyke's fingers away from me, but Jack is still holding my arms.

"Someone google it," Jack says. "We need to get to the bottom of this."

Jack's steely eyes stare into mine but I know he doesn't really see me. That is, he doesn't see the person I am *to me*, only the person I am *to him*. And to him I am a party trick, another beer bottle to balance on his chin.

10

FAUNA

The forest is full of whispers, frantic voices traveling from root to root.

"...They will bring us all down with them..."

"...For millennia, we have offered up ourselves, keeping the peace, but we can't go on like this..."

"...The day is soon here, when it will be too late..."

"...We have to find a way to tell them, to make them understand..."

"...No matter what it takes."

II

FLORA

I FEEL MY CHEST TIGHTEN.

"Let me go." My voice is trembling, but Jack only continues to stare at me, the corner of his mouth turning upward in a crooked smirk. He is still holding my arms in a firm grip, his breath reeking of alcohol.

Aaron grabs an empty beer bottle and offers it to Jack. "Come on, do that thing again, on your chin."

But Jack ignores him. My arms are hurting so badly my eyes well up. "Let me go," I repeat, louder this time. I try to yank myself free, but Jack just squeezes my arms tighter, tighter, with that smirk of his.

"First we need to take a good look at what you've got," he snorts.

"You're hurting me," I say. With one last pull, I break free. But Jack grabs my waist and with his free hand starts pulling at my t-shirt. I hear a girl's voice from somewhere behind me. "He's out of control! Someone should get his parents!"

"What are you doing?" I shriek, yanking on my t-shirt to keep it down. "Stop it!"

My voice is drowned out by Seth and Tyke, chanting, "Get it off, get it off!"

I try to push Jack away as glass bottles bump against my arm and crash to the floor. I can't believe this is happening as I feel his strong arm around me, his hand fumbling and groping my chest. "Take your hands off me!" I insist.

The cheers are filling the kitchen now—"Get it off, get it off, get it off!"—and before I can stop him, Jack rips the t-shirt apart, between *I am* and *here*, and pulls it off me.

I try to shield myself in only my tan cotton bra, feeling their gaze on my scarred skin. Fauna's favorite t-shirt is now ripped and lying on the floor. There's nowhere I can go. "Get away from me," I shout. I turn around and around, my heart pounding. "Get away!" I can't see Aaron anywhere. Tears make everything blurry: Jack, the kitchen, the crowd, a girl pushing a boy.

Someone pulls at my bra strap while they continue chanting, "Get it off, get it off." I sink down to the floor, my back against the island, but Jack doesn't seem satisfied. That smirk is still on his face.

"What's the matter?" he mocks. "I thought you wanted to investigate your—" He bends to pull my hair to the side, his hand brushing against my shoulder, making me wince. "—Your Lichtenberg figures." He makes it sound dirty.

"Don't touch me," I scowl, trying to keep from crying.

But Jack is twice my size. He could lift me up and carry me away like a rag doll.

Through the murmur and the cheering, I hear Aaron's voice. "She's in here."

"Flora?" Carl calls out. He fights his way through the crowd until he sees me on the floor. He crouches down next to me. "You okay?"

I nod slightly.

He turns to Jack. "What have you done to her?" He takes a step closer to him, boring a hole into him through his eyes. "Whatever you think you're doing, it ends now."

Jack stares at Carl, like he's having a hard time processing what he just said. "Come on, man, we were just having fun." He lets out a chuckle, but no one is laughing anymore. Somewhere in the kitchen, a girl is crying in heavy sobs.

"Is this your idea of having fun? Are you insane?" Carl gestures to the raised smartphones all around us. "And if this goes viral, you can kiss college goodbye. No more football for you."

Jack's smirk is gone. His bloodshot eyes wander over the crowd, widening like he's surprised to see everyone. He stops, shifts his weight as if considering his options, then motions to the crowd. "Everyone delete it now." He nods to Seth and Tyke. "Make sure it's all gone."

Turning to me, Carl unbuttons his checkered shirt, revealing a white t-shirt underneath. His hands tremble, and I have never seen the look of rage in his eyes. He takes off the shirt and hands it to me. Wiping my tears, I put it on quickly, not bothering to match the buttons correctly. I just want to get out of here.

I crawl over the bottles and beer puddles to get Fauna's shirt, but Carl picks it up first, then grabs my hand to pull me to my feet.

My knees are shaking and my skirt has wriggled up over my thighs. I pull it down. The crowd is starting to disperse, and Seth and Tyke are checking people's cell phones.

"Let's get out of here," Carl says.

Behind us Jack mutters, "That's one flower that needs to be picked."

Carl stops. He exhales and releases my hand, then turns around and *thumps* his fist into Jack's face. The force of it strikes Jack down on the spot. He's now the one on the floor, blinking like he can't believe what just happened as blood wells from his cracked lips.

"If you ever . . ." Carl's voice is shaking. "Ever . . ." He leans over Jack. "Ever . . . touch her again." He turns to the crowd, the ones who are still here, a few smartphones still raised. "That's something you can post wherever the hell you want."

Suddenly, I can't stop the tears. I rush out of the kitchen and down the stairs, not caring that I shove into people. There's an octopus in my stomach making me feel nauseous, like I need to throw up.

Out on the driveway, I stop and bend over, heaving with

my head in my hands. The cool night air, scented by lavender, gently strokes my hair.

"Wait, Flora." It's Carl.

I don't want to turn around, don't want him to see me like this. Shaking my head, all I can say is, "I need to get home."

"But Flora—"

With my back still turned to him to hide my tears, I quickly walk away, struggling to fasten the shirt correctly with my trembling hands. I can't get it out of my head, how they looked at me. And Carl—I can't believe he saw me like that. I tuck my hands into the sleeves of his shirt, making sure every inch of my lightning marks are covered. He saw it. All of it. The freak I am.

Carl calls my name, but I start running, desperate to leave the Dunnes' street behind me. Carl's shirt is so big it flaps against my back with my every stride. The houses with their bright porch lights are a blur as I pass them. Running helps ease the nausea, though. Deep breaths, in and out. As I pound the pavement faster and faster, I feel the octopus crawl away.

When I reach our house, light flickers from the kitchen window behind the branches of the oak tree and I know that Mom is back. I stop to wipe my tears. Above me, the leaves rustle in the breeze and there is that strange tingle in my skin again—like an echo of the fingers touching me, stroking me. I shiver and run across our driveway, then up the porch steps. I fling the screen and front door open. "Mom?" My voice breaks the word into two jagged pieces.

She is sitting at the kitchen table, her head resting in her arms. She looks up as I enter.

"Did you have fun?" She smiles, but her eyes are red and swollen. "At the party?"

She looks so hopeful, and I swallow hard; maybe she won't notice I've been crying. She seems distracted, only half waiting for my response.

"Uh huh." I nod.

Mom's smile widens. "Thanks for coming home early. I wanted to . . ." She looks around the kitchen like she's searching for the right words in the porcelain sink, the wooden cabinets, the worn tabletop of the kitchen table. Her smile fades. "I wanted to say I'm sorry. I know Fauna's seizure wasn't your fault."

She reminds me of a withered flower, the way she sits slumped in her chair. My heart aching, I go over to her and bend down to put my arms around her. "How is she?"

Mom reaches for me and pulls me close. "Same as before." She wipes her eyes with the back of her hand. "I just got so scared, Flora."

"Me too." My lip trembles, I can't help it, and Mom puts her hand on my cheek.

"You sure you're okay, honey?" She nudges the sleeve of Carl's shirt. "Where did you get that?"

"Um . . ." I mumble and force a smile. "I spilled something on my t-shirt." I quickly follow it with, "I'm tired, I think I'll go to bed."

Mom nods and lets go of me. "Okay."

I walk up the creaking stairs to my bedroom, where I sink down with my back against the door. In the familiar darkness of my room, I can finally breathe. I unbutton Carl's shirt and trace the lightning marks on my arms, my chest, my neck—the slight irregularities in my skin barely percep- tible. But I know they're there. I can feel them, the tender scars branching out like an imprint of the flash of lightning. I can't help but rub my arms, like I could scratch off the memories burning in my mind—the chants of "Get it off," the eyes glaring at me, the laughter, the fingers stroking my skin—like I could erase the sadness from Mom's eyes, erase Fauna's seizure, her wheelchair, her empty gaze.

Get it off.

Like I could bring her back.

But it's no use.

Quiet, I tell myself. I can't let Mom hear me sobbing.

Outside my bedroom window the night breeze wails through the branches of the oak tree. Up by the road, a laugh penetrates the night, followed by muffled voices. They remind me of Jack Dunne and his stupid friends.

I reach for the covers on my bed and pull them off and over me. Curled up on the floor, I can pretend that we've built a fort like we used to when we were little, Fauna and I, where nothing could harm us.

More laughter seeps in from outside, and then raised voices, someone shouting. I can't make out the words, but I don't want to.

"It's alright, Fauna," I whisper, "stay here with me."

12

Fauna

Please, don't.

Please, don't.

But the axe is already biting me.

Please, please, please.

No one hears my cries, only the night, the forest, the trees all whispering the same thing.

". . . This is the only way, the only language they will understand . . ."

". . . The language of steel and blood . . ."

". . . There's nothing else to do, nothing else to say, it is too late."

13

FLORA

THE SCREEN DOOR SHUTS WITH A BANG BEHIND ME, but I hear it open again as I hurry down the steps of the porch. The concern cracks through Mom's words. "You'll be alright?"

I turn around. "Don't worry, Mom. I've opened up the Book Nook, like, a million times."

Standing in the doorway, under the faded sign reading *Pine Ridge Farm*, she wraps the bathrobe tighter around her. I glimpse the nightgown clinging to her thin body, the contours of her collarbone under her skin. I knew she hadn't been eating enough. A surge of tenderness runs through me. "I'll pick up groceries on my way home," I offer.

"I'll join you after I've visited Fauna . . ." Mom turns quiet, her gaze wandering from my shoulder to the emptiness I always carry beside me.

I nod. "Okay, later then." But she isn't listening. She slowly stretches out her hand, pointing to something behind me. I turn around.

The scarred oak tree—Fauna's and my oak tree—is draped with toilet paper on its beautiful branches and twisted around its trunk.

"What the hell?" I run across the driveway, the gravel crunching under my feet. "Who did this?" And then I notice the gleaming axe and the gasoline can and the empty beer cans scattered among the roots. "No, no, no," I mutter as I crawl around in the grass gathering the sour-smelling cans, cold against my fingers and wet with morning dew. One is half full and when I pick it up, the suds drizzle to the ground, splashing yellow stains on my white sneakers. The pungent smell of gasoline is everywhere, stinging my eyes.

Mom picks up the gas can and shakes her head. Carrying it toward the driveway, she suddenly lets out a scream. Her pained wail penetrates my bones, the same way it did on the day of the accident. I follow her frozen gaze up into the oak tree and am choked into silence.

Among the branches and strips of toilet paper is a boy.

He seems trapped by the branches crisscrossing his chest, entangled in a mess of twigs and leaves. He is staring down at us with wide-open, bloodshot eyes, as if he is surprised to see us. His pale, bluish face is full of scratches, and his arms hang limp by his sides.

I want to back away, but my feet are stuck, my whole body heavy like a block of stone. My lightning marks are tingling, stinging, burning along my arms, my neck, my chest.

Mom has stopped screaming, but I can hear her voice as if it's coming from far away. "My God, my God."

In the boy's forehead, the scratches form an uneven but distinct X, as if it's been carved into his skin deliberately. The jagged wounds, dried and blackened, have bled crooked lines across his face. Still, I recognize him. Those cracked lips, those broad shoulders in the ripped blue-and-white varsity jacket, those large hands like drooping flowers.

"Do you know him?" Mom is by my side, holding me up. I cling to her, or is she the one clinging to me?

"Jack," I whisper. "Jack Dunne."

What I'm seeing can't be real. *Is this some sick joke?* I wonder. It's not Halloween, it's the middle of June. My blood pulses and rushes to my head. And then I feel nausea, dizziness.

"We need to call an ambulance . . . or the police," Mom stutters.

I pull my phone from my pocket, but I can barely see the numbers as tears blur my vision.

"Nine, one, one, what's your emergency?" The voice, a woman's, sounds like it's coming from a dark abyss. I search for the right words, but they all seem wrong.

"Jack . . . a boy from school . . ." I start, the brutal, bleeding reality of it hitting me. "Jack is stuck in our tree. He's . . . He's not moving . . ."

"What is your location?" The woman sounds unnaturally calm. *Didn't she hear what I just said?*

"Pine . . ." I can barely remember our address. "Twenty-five Pine Ridge Road. In Derwyn." The air seems like mud I have to force down. "We just found him. He seems trapped somehow . . . in our tree. And he's not . . . he's not . . ." I can't make myself say it. *Alive. Breathing.*

Gasping for air—which Jack can't do because it's clear that Jack's not breathing—I look up at the tree, at Jack, and I cannot bear it. I have to bring him down from there. Maybe it's not too late. Maybe I can save him.

"Is there someone with you?" The woman is still calm. "Is there an adult I can speak to?"

I hand the phone to Mom and run into the arms of the oak tree. My lightning marks remember the last time I climbed it; I can feel my skin burning as if I am set on fire. Below me Mom is giving directions to the dispatcher and pacing back and forth over the gravel. She motions for me to come down, but I am already balancing on the branch above him, confused. There's no rope holding him up, nothing but twigs and branches.

The sirens are already screaming up our street. Carefully, I bend down to get closer. Around Jack's neck are twisted twigs, in a strange noose of sprigs and leaves, and the branches are wrapped around his torso like arms squeezing him, crushing him.

My skin is pulsating, and the lightning scars on my arms are bright red, like the day I got them. My hands are suddenly shaking so badly I can barely hold on to the tree.

Flora!

I look down. Our whole front yard is flooded with police officers, firefighters, paramedics, and neighbors.

Flora!

There it is again. But it's no one from below. It seems to come from inside of me, from the burning, the throbbing in my skin.

Floor-ra. Floor-ra.

Tears spring to my eyes again. I remember her voice, my butterfly of a little sister, searching for me in the tall grass, the insects buzzing around me, the caterpillar measuring the edge of my sketchbook. And then I hear Mom.

"Flora, come down from there. What are you doing?"

I realize I am standing on the branch, my arms raised in front of me.

A broad-shouldered police officer starts to climb up. "Miss, please come down from the tree." He is already halfway to Jack, maneuvering the tree's limbs with surprising agility for a man in his forties. He looks up at me and frowns, his voice deep and commanding. "This is a crime scene."

My skin is still burning.

Flooo-ra.

Fumbling, I reach for another branch, and there's that octopus again in my stomach, releasing its nauseating tentacles.

I have to get down.

As fast as I can, my hands remembering every crevice in the tree, I follow the jagged lightning scar in the trunk until I am standing on the ground, with the wide trunk between me and the mayhem in our front yard.

Swiping my tears away, I gaze up into the oak's majestic crown and see the morning light breaking through the leaves. My sister's voice replays in my mind. *Floor-ra.* It was so . . . real. As if she was right beside me, sitting in the tree like before her accident.

The police officer crouches next to Jack's body. "It's too late," he shouts down to his colleague on the ground, a thirty-something woman with a black ponytail. "There's nothing we can do for him."

The female officer waves to a firefighter who steps up and leans a metal ladder against the trunk. Another police officer, wearing latex gloves and carrying a shoulder bag, makes his way up.

The nausea forces me to bend over as I recall the police officer's words: *It's too late.* I close my eyes and inhale the warm morning air, force it down, fill my lungs with the earthy scent of grass and leaves.

"Miss Reed?"

I look up into the grave face of the broad-shouldered police officer, the one who has just climbed down from the tree.

"Yes." My voice is so weak, I can barely hear it myself.

"I am Chief of Police Batista." He flips his notepad open

and clicks a ballpoint pen. "I need to ask you a couple of questions, if that's alright?" He pauses and looks at me, and there's a familiar concern in his eyes. *She is that girl.* I realize he has already been briefed by someone about our tragic backstory.

I nod, and a trace of a smile appears in Chief Batista's eyes.

"How old are you?" he asks.

"I turned seventeen in March." I notice a small twig stuck in my hair and pull it out, then brush pieces of tree bark from my wrinkled t-shirt and shorts.

Chief Batista scribbles in his notepad, looking tiny in his large hand. "Can you tell me what happened this morning?"

I look for Mom, but I can't find her anywhere in the commotion.

"I was on my way to the Book Nook to open it up for the day." Suddenly, I see Carl in the crowd. I am about to call for him, but he has already spotted me. His eyes widen, wandering from me to the lifeless body of Jack, entwined in the oak tree and surrounded by police officers. I wish I could speak to him, tell him everything, but he turns and dashes up our driveway, disappearing behind the hawthorn hedge.

The female officer is putting up yellow tape around the oak tree that says POLICE LINE DO NOT CROSS in black block letters. At the foot of the tree, another police officer is taking pictures of the crime scene.

Chief Batista ushers me away. "The Book Nook . . ." he

prompts me, flipping open his notepad again. "That is The Wee Reed Book Nook, your mom's bookshop, right?"

"Yes," I say. "I help her out during the summer."

"Chief," the female officer says. "Crime scene investigators say they're done in the tree. They didn't find much."

"Thanks, Officer Herrera." Chief Batista motions to the firefighters waiting below the tree. "They can bring him down."

Chief Batista turns back to me. "What were you doing in the tree?"

I don't want to look at Jack—at his blood-streaked face, his body trapped among the branches—but I can't help it. The bruising on his lips and cheek where Carl planted his fist seems even more purple against his pale skin.

"I tried to get him down, but I couldn't find a rope, or . . . anything. I don't know. . ." The tingling and burning in my skin is finally starting to subside, and I wrap my arms around myself, suddenly cold in the morning breeze.

The firefighters work with a handsaw and loppers to cut Jack loose. They shout instructions back and forth as they slowly untangle him, leaves and twigs raining to the ground. When they finally lift Jack out of the tree, one of them carries him like a doll over his shoulder.

I can't watch anymore as the octopus reaches its tentacles through my insides again.

Chief Batista leans close. "How are you feeling? You alright?"

I nod and he turns the page in his notepad.

"Did you know the deceased?"

He said it. *The deceased.* "He goes to—" I look down at the ground and shake my head. "I mean, he *went* to my school, but we didn't really hang out."

Chief Batista frowns. "No?"

I shrug. I don't want to tell him about the invisible wall between me and other people. I'm certain that Chief Batista, in his white-shirt-black-tie assertiveness, would never understand how it feels to be *that girl*. And I definitely don't want to tell him what happened last night at the party.

Almost as if he could read my mind, Chief Batista asks, "Where were you last night?"

I feel as though I'm being led into a trap. "At the end-of-year party at the Dunnes' place."

Chief Batista clears his throat and jots more notes. "Do you have someone who can confirm this?"

"Yes—" I hesitate. "Everyone at the party." I don't say *everyone who saw Jack Dunne rip my t-shirt to shreds*. I don't say *Carl, who punched him in the face*.

Chief Batista scratches his chin, the stubble rasping against his fingers. "Do you know of anyone who might have wanted to hurt Jack?"

I shake my head. It's not lying. I know that Carl would never do something like this, not to Jack, not to anyone. Carl with his warm chestnut eyes, his deep dimples, his backpack properly worn on both shoulders. But then I remember the rage in his eyes when he struck Jack down without any hesitation. I start to shiver, the warmth and brightness of the summer morning eclipsed by the cold that seems to seep from my bones.

"Are you interrogating my daughter?" Mom asks, coming up beside me and wrapping me in a red knit blanket. Mom's hair is still a messy copper halo around her face, but she is now dressed in jeans and her gray Philadelphia Eagles sweatshirt. "She's just a kid. She shouldn't be interrogated without a parent present." Mom has that wrinkle between her eyes we used to fear. "I refuse to let her answer any more of your questions."

Chief Batista bows his head in a sort of stiff nod. "I'm sorry." For a second he looks like a boy being scolded by his mom, even though he and Mom are probably about the same age. "I've never seen anything like this." He motions to the body of Jack lying on the stretcher. "That poor boy."

"Well, this is *my* girl, and if you want to talk to her, you better ask me first." Mom clutches me tightly, like she is trying to show Chief Batista exactly which girl she is speaking of.

"You!" We all turn to the deep voice. Among the paramedics I recognize Mr. Dunne, shoving an EMT out of his way. He runs toward me, his dark hair a mess, his blue shirt untucked. "I saw the video. I know what you did!"

I pull back, but two police officers are already restraining him. "You and that boy!" he shouts, struggling against the officers.

Behind Mr. Dunne I see Mrs. Dunne leaning over Jack's still body, her head on his chest and her shoulders shaking. Her ash blond hair is spread out over her son like a shroud. I want to look away, but I can't.

"I know what—" Mr. Dunne manages to get his hand free from the officer holding him back, and points at me. "You did!"

"Come, honey." Mom drags me across the driveway and pulls me behind the hawthorn hedge. "Go to the Book Nook. Don't come back until—"

Mr. Dunne's booming voice cuts her off. "Where is she going, damn it? Take your hands off me!"

I drop the blanket and run between the fire truck and police cars lining Pine Ridge Road, past the Owens' house and the curious neighbors streaming up the street. Before I turn the corner to Maple Street, I turn back to see the thin figure of my mother, swimming in her loose sweatshirt, frantically talking to the crowd. The police officers, the Dunnes. She is facing all of them alone.

And then I remember.

I exhale slowly, my heart aching.

She has done all of this before. Sort of. Only that was another day, another kid, a young girl lying motionless under the tree.

14

FAUNA

Flora, Flora.

Do you hear me?

I am here.

I can feel the steel eating into my flesh, the twigs breaking.

"Please, no one else," I beg the trees. "No more bloodshed. I will take the pain, the jagged teeth cutting me, just no one else, please, please."

But there is only silence coming through the roots.

15

FLORA

ON MY WAY TO THE BOOK NOOK, I TEXT CARL.

They'll be looking for you

I keep the phone in my hand, checking for messages every other step. At the end of Maple Street, a white van comes screeching through the intersection, *The Philadelphia Examiner* written across its side in black calligraphy.

I hear the van come to a stop with a roar, back up, and then a guy's voice behind me. "Hi, do you know the way to Pine Ridge Road?"

My heart begins to race. I turn and point. "Just follow this street and you'll see it."

"Thanks," he says. The engine of the van rumbles, then revs as it drives away.

I check my phone again. No answer.

I dash across the intersection and continue running under the canopy of trees lining the street. Panting, I force the warm morning air into my lungs, feeling that strange tingling in my lightning marks rise and fall, like a tidal wave of fire. I text Carl again.

> They know what happened at
> the party

Looking downward, I bump into someone, a middle-aged man in a dark suit holding his phone to his ear. I step back. "Oh, sorry."

He doesn't answer, just frowns at me, then shifts his gaze to my scarred arms. A look of recognition cross his face before he hastens around the corner. "It was her," I hear him say. "Yes, that girl."

WHEN I REACH the store, I press my shoulder to the emerald door and turn the key. Once inside, I lock the door again. The stranger's voice echoes in my head—*It was her*—and then Mr. Dunne's—*I know what you did.* Does he think I had something to do with Jack's death? He must have seen a video of Carl punching Jack. I guess I was in it too, half-dressed, a mess. I can't help letting out a groan as I sink to the floor behind the counter. I don't want to think about any of it—Jack in the tree, Chief Batista's interrogation, how I left Mom in the chaos of our front yard.

My thoughts are interrupted by a soft *thud* upstairs—a

book falling over, or maybe a muffled footstep. I quietly crawl across the floorboards to the bookshelf next to the counter. I reach under it and close my fingers around the smooth handle of the baseball bat we keep hidden for emergencies.

I pull it out slowly, careful not to let it tap against the floor. With my other hand, I reach for the counter and gingerly pull myself up.

I tiptoe to the other end of our small shop, checking behind every shelf with the bat raised in front of me. Then I make my way up the stairs.

One, two, *creak*. Damn it.

Three steps more and I can see the second floor. Someone is lying on the old floral couch. My heart pounds against my ribs as I tighten my grip on the bat. I take a deep breath. "Who's there?"

There's a pause, then, "Flora?"

I exhale and lower the bat.

"Carl? What are you doing here?" I climb the last few stairs. "Why didn't you answer my messages?"

He ignores my questions and instead lets out a sigh. "Thank God you're safe."

I plop down next to him. "How did you get in?"

"The back door." He smiles, but this time it's a dimpleless smile that fades quickly. "I picked the lock."

"You what?"

He shrugs and shakes his head. "It's not that hard."

I can't help staring at him. *He knows how to pick locks?* "The police are going to look for you, you know."

He tugs at the collar of his dark blue shirt, like he's feeling trapped in it. "Yeah, I guess. That's why I figured I need to lie low for a while." He slumps with his elbows against the threadbare knees of his jeans. "The last thing I need is the police asking questions."

I wonder what he means, if he might be referring to something that happened before he was placed in foster care with the Owens.

"But you didn't do it!" I swallow hard, telling my stupid brain not to think it, but I say it anyway. "Right?"

Carl jumps up. "Of course not!" He moves toward the window, shaking his head. "How could I?" He turns to me. "What *was* that back there? Who could have done such a thing?"

I stare down at the weapon still in my hands. "It was awful," I whisper.

Carl gently takes the bat from me and leans it against the couch. "I'm sorry. It must have been a shock . . . finding him like that."

"I tried to . . ." Tears well up again. "I tried to help him."

Carl smiles tenderly, revealing a dimple in his cheek. "That's so you, Flora. Even after what he did to you."

I look away and let my eyes wander over the uneven rows and piles of books in the crammed bookshelves, not wanting to remember this morning. I feel Carl sit back down next to me. Without saying anything, he reaches to pick a tiny leaf out of my hair, fumbling as he tries to untangle it. I can't help but smile through the tears at his concentrated gaze, his trembling fingers, determined to free this remnant of the crime scene from my golden strands.

"Thanks for standing up for me," I whisper, noticing the string of purple bruises along his knuckles. I can't bring myself to add "against Jack."

But Carl's focus is elsewhere. "There!" he says, triumphantly holding the leaf. Then he grows serious. "Flora, I—"

We both flinch at the sound of voices outside. A few seconds later, there is a loud banging on the front door.

I wipe my eyes and check the time on my phone. "Oh crap! It's way past ten. We should be open."

"Right," Carl says, rubbing his temples and giving me a sly smile. "Someone must be desperate for a book."

I start for the stairs. "Wait. What are you going to do?"

He shrugs. "Can I hang around here for a while . . . just until I have to go to Math Wizards?"

The banging on the door continues, and I hurry to the stairs. "Okay," I say, "but don't scare the customers."

Carl lets out a chuckle and nods toward the bat. "Not unless I have to."

I shoot him a smirk, then run downstairs. Immediately, I freeze. Mr. Dunne is peering through the glass in the front door. He pounds the door again so hard that the glass rattles. "I need to talk to you," he bellows. "Open up, damn it!"

My mind races. *Should I call the police?* No, I need to warn Carl. But Mr. Dunne's eyes are following my every move. I have no choice but to walk across the shop and unlock the door. The happy jingle of the doorbell seems terribly inappropriate.

"Mr. Dunne," I say, hoping Carl hears me. "I am so very sorry for your—"

But Mr. Dunne pushes past me. "Where is he?"

"Who?" I ask as he starts darting between the aisles.

He stops and wipes his forehead. "That friend of yours, the boy who assaulted my . . ." He exhales and it sounds like a sob. "My son." His beige pants are sprinkled with mud stains, and his blue shirt is dark under the armpits.

"Mr. Dunne," I repeat a bit louder. "Let me say how . . ." But his desperate eyes, his panting, his shaking hands, the red-brown spot on his chest—blood, his son's blood. I realize in that moment that there's nothing I can say to ease his pain. "I am so, so, sorry," I manage, my voice barely a whisper.

Even though he is a head taller than me, his wide eyes and creased brow remind me of a begging child. "Tell your friend that I need to talk to him. Please, I need to know what happened."

I swallow hard and nod. His grief seems to shift between rage and sorrow right before my eyes.

He suddenly notices the stairs. "What's up there?"

"Just more books," I say, trying to sound casual.

Mr. Dunne squints. "Just books, huh?" He walks over to the stairs and peers up. "Can I take a look?"

I open my mouth to say no, to give some excuse about water damage or wet paint, but he is already on his way up.

"Wait!" I blurt out, following him. "It's pretty messy."

But he bounds up nonetheless. I expect him to see Carl straightaway, but as I reach the second floor, I see that the space is empty. *Did he manage to sneak down the stairs and out the back door?*

Mr. Dunne inspects the stuffy, compact room, the bookshelves, even our old floral couch and kitchenette. "More books" is all he says with a sigh before clomping downstairs again.

I am about to follow him, but then I notice the window. I scurry across the room toward the faint breeze. *I don't remember leaving the window open.*

The doorbell jingles and on the sidewalk below me I can see Mr. Dunne leave. The bald spot in his dark hair and his wide shoulders don't seem nearly as intimidating from this vantage point. I feel a surge of pity for him. The way he walks, his head bent, reminds me of Mom the day of the accident. With my forehead pressed against the glass, I watch his slumped figure disappear around the corner.

I push the window closed and turn around. As I scan the empty room, I think, *That whopping boy! He comes and goes as he pleases, like he could walk through walls.*

16

FAUNA

It's like I can sense what will happen; time is blurring together.

Like I can remember in all directions.

Shadows taking form in my mind: branches reaching, creaking; bodies struggling, choking.

Blood, fire, soil, water.

A desert of ashes.

I have to find a way to warn my sister; I have to warn them all.

17

FLORA

TWO BOYS, AROUND SEVEN AND EIGHT, TUMBLE into the Book Nook after peeking through the shop window for several minutes, pushing each other like they were daring one another to go first.

"Hey there." I force a smile. "Did you need help finding something?"

Hesitantly, they come up to the counter. The shorter one looks up at me with round eyes. "Was there a murder at your house?" He stumbles on *murder*, like the gruesome word doesn't fit in his mouth.

The other boy, the taller one, chimes in. "Or was it a suicide?" He puts his elbows on the counter and leans in, scratching his tousled hair, like he's playing detective. "Did you see him?"

The smaller boy's eyes widen. "Was he like . . ." He crinkles his nose. ". . . all blue and bloody?"

As they stare at me, waiting for an answer, I can tell

they've translated overheard conversations between adults into their childish world of games and plays, cops and robbers, hide-and-seek, where everyone at the end brushes it all off and goes home to dinner.

I lean down on the counter, forcing another smile. "I think you should find your—"

A woman storms into the shop. "I told you boys not to wander off!" She grabs them by the arms and throws me an apologetic look. She lingers on me for a moment, then pulls the boys out the door with her.

It is not until the doorbell has stopped jingling that I realize why the woman hesitated when she saw me. She must have been thinking, *You're that girl.*

MOM ARRIVES AT the Book Nook just before closing time.

"I'm sorry I couldn't come earlier." She's panting like she's been running. The lines in her forehead tell me about her day, the turmoil she had to manage in our yard-turned-crime-scene. Still she asks me, "You alright?"

"Yeah." I nod. "Not much happening here." I don't want to burden her with Mr. Dunne's visit.

Mom comes around the counter and hugs me. "I'm so sorry, honey. This must be terrible for you." She looks into my eyes. "He was in your grade, wasn't he?"

I want to tell her everything, about Jack, the party, Carl,

but my throat feels tight and I don't know where to start.

Mom turns to the window and sighs heavily. "What is *he* doing here?"

A police car has just pulled up and Chief Batista hops out. The jingle of the bell counters his deep voice as he enters the store. "Just one question!"

Mom crosses her arms. "I thought we were done."

"For Flora." The chief's eyes dart between me and Mom. "If it's alright with you, ma'am."

Mom turns to me and raises her eyebrows. "You okay with that?"

My mouth is suddenly dry. "Yeah."

He steps closer, and I can smell his balmy aftershave. "Did you see something else in the tree? Something . . ." He searches for words without taking his eyes off me. ". . . unusual?"

I can't shake the feeling that Chief Batista is trying to lure me into a trap. What could I tell him? *That my lightning marks tingled and burned when I climbed the tree? That I imagined hearing my sister's voice and it was so real that I nearly thought she was there with me?* It would all sound completely insane. I shake my head. "Just the way he was caught in the branches." A shiver runs through me. "Sort of intertwined with the tree."

Mom puts her arm around me and pulls me close. "She's already told you all she knows."

Chief Batista raises his hand. "Just one more question,

please." His eyes bore deep into mine. "Do you know where Carl Nielsen might be?"

I hesitate. "No, why?"

"I'd like to ask him a couple of questions." Chief Batista's eyes lock me in place. "Just to get another eyewitness statement."

I struggle not to look away from his intense gaze, then Chief Batista shifts his weight and lets his shoulders drop.

"I saw the video, Miss Reed." His voice is surprisingly soft.

"What video?" Mom asks. "The one Mike Dunne was talking about?"

A sudden ache throbs in my stomach.

Chief Batista pulls his phone from his belt and holds it up in front of us. I don't want Mom to see this, but there is no escape.

The image is blurry and shaky, but I recognize myself on the floor by the island in the Dunnes' kitchen, trying to shield myself, my arms around my almost-naked upper body. It's only a couple of seconds before Carl fills the frame, but I can feel Mom flinch and squeeze me tighter.

The ache in my stomach throbs more intensely.

The screen has turned murky with voices laughing and mumbling. "Here he comes . . . are you getting this? Oh, man . . ." Then we see Carl take off his shirt. The video goes off focus, capturing a few onlookers and then back to Jack, mumbling something inaudible.

And then it happens: Carl turns and punches Jack in the

face, knocking him to the floor as the crowd ooohs and aaahs. Then the video ends.

Chief Batista lowers his phone, his eyes searching mine.

"What happened at that party, Miss Reed? It's obvious that you were . . ." He pauses. "You were assaulted in some way, weren't you?"

Mom sniffles beside me. "Why didn't you tell me? Who did that to you? Was it Jack?" Her fingers dig into my arm.

Chief Batista leans in close. "Is that why Carl punched him?"

I pull back, shaking my head. "He didn't kill him."

Chief Batista steps even closer. "But I do need to speak to him."

Mom is still clinging to me. "Tell me what happened. Tell me!"

The ache in my stomach turns into a burning pain. It all comes flooding back: the chanting voices, Jack ripping my t-shirt, his hands groping my chest.

"I don't want to talk about it!" I break free from Mom's embrace and run to the door, yanking it open to that damn have-a-good-day jingle. Before it closes, I hear Mom say, "Can you imagine what she's been through? Could you just leave her alone for one minute?"

Tears burn my eyes as I run down the street. The cars and the row of shops and the linden trees lining the street blur into a mess of colors, turning it all into a flowing water-color painting.

I FIND FAUNA in the garden of White Oak Manor. She sits in her wheelchair under a maple tree and I rush right past Abigail on the patio, throwing myself down on the grass by Fauna's feet.

"I can't . . . I just can't," I gasp. My stomach is still throbbing and I'm completely out of breath.

Fauna's forget-me-not eyes are staring up into the sky, looking as though they're cut from the same blue fabric.

"Please, look at me," I beg, my words sounding like sobs.

But she just sits there, her pale hands resting in her lap. I grab them, feeling her skinny legs under my arms. "Please, Fauna."

Yesterday, right before her seizure, she looked at me. I know she recognized me, that she knew it was me. For a second, she was there with me. I had my little sister again.

"I got so scared yesterday," I tell her, squeezing her thin fingers. "Please, Fauna, you must never leave me." The tears are back and I don't even try to wipe them away. "Promise, that you'll never leave me."

Fauna's eyes remain fixed above her.

"I couldn't bear it if you were gone." I throw my arms around her, wheelchair and all. Her ginger hair smells faintly of roses.

Over Fauna's shoulder, I see Abigail pacing back and

forth on the patio, pointing to the lawn. And then I see it. Behind Fauna's wheelchair is a trail of dandelions and daisies blossoming like golden coins in the grass, creating a floral carpet rolled out behind her. The wide lawn spreads out in a uniform short stubble, but oddly, it is greener, longer, and thicker among the flowers and around Fauna's wheelchair—almost as if it's reaching for her.

18

FAUNA

Flowers at my roots, stars at my head, fireflies buzzing at my fingertips.

Birds on my shoulders, squirrels nestled by my neck.

Summer's breeze caressing my skin, winter's snow a coat around me.

For thousands of years, this has been our heritage, our birthright, the timetable of trees.

Without our birthright, what are we?

When it is stolen from us, chopped up, and burned?

What are we?

19

FLORA

"WHAT THE—?" I EXCLAIM, BUT THEN I NOTICE Abigail's frantic waving from the patio. Carefully I let go of Fauna and hurry across the lawn to the shaded area at the back of White Oak Manor.

"So you see it too?" Abigail whispers like she's afraid the flowers might hear her. "I swear, I thought I was going mad."

All I can think about is how small Fauna looks out there in the garden, with no one beside her. "Maybe we better get her inside," I suggest.

Abigail's chin trembles. "I'm not going out there!"

"It's just flowers," I assure her. I cross the lawn, stepping gingerly along the flower trail leading to Fauna. I can feel my lightning marks pulsating, not as much as they did in the oak tree, but still.

"Let's go inside, Fauna." I unlock her wheelchair and pull her around while Abigail waits on the patio, her hand now on her chest. As I push Fauna toward her, Abigail's eyes widen.

"Look at it," she mutters.

When I reach the stone floor of the patio, I turn around. *Am I imagining it?* I witness the flowers closing their petals and bowing their heads into the grass. The strange tingling in my lightning marks subsides until I can't feel it anymore. And then the lawn is green again, like nothing happened.

ON OUR WAY to Fauna's room, Abigail turns to me.

"There's something else. I hardly believed my eyes at first, but—" She stops in the doorway and gasps. "My Lord! It's even worse than before."

I peer in and see that the geraniums have grown to twice their size since yesterday, a pink and fuchsia firework of blooms.

"Black magic!" Abigail shrieks, her eyes fierce. She backs away and rushes out the door, leaving me with Fauna.

I shake my head, taken aback by Abigail's outburst. Then I push my sister to her favorite spot by the window. "Here, Fauna," I say, patting her shoulder, "just how you like it."

My sister sits in the same position she always does, her thin hands in her lap, her eyes staring off into the distance. If only I could shake her out of it. Following her gaze to the garden, I wonder what Carl meant by saying he needed to lie low for a while. I figured he would avoid the police, but I haven't heard from him all day. *Is he thinking of running away?* My chest suddenly feels heavy, like a weight is pressing me down.

There's a *ping* from my phone. It's Mom.

> How are you doing? I'm
> picking up your favorite sushi
> for dinner. You home soon?
> Love you.

> On my way, I answer.

But I don't want to leave Fauna. I want to stay in her blossoming kingdom instead of going home to where Jack—. But the thought of Mom sitting alone at the kitchen table, staring out at the oak tree, is too much.

I bend down to put my arms around my sister. "I'll see you soon, okay?"

From the corner of my eye, I see Rhonda from reception appear in the doorframe.

"What happened?" she asks. "Abigail just told me she refuses to work with Fauna anymore."

My heart drops. "What? Can she do that?"

Rhonda smooths her blue gingham blouse. "I'll take it up with the director . . . and discuss it with your mother."

I think of Mom's tired eyes, the creases in her forehead. "Please don't. It's okay. Is there someone else who can take over?"

Rhonda's eyes linger on Fauna. "Well, I can cover the evening shift today."

I dash over to her. "Thank you," I say, giving her a hug. "I really appreciate it." She squeezes me hard, enveloping me in her black curls and faint scent of peppermint.

"I heard what happened this morning." She grimaces. "I'm sorry."

I bite my lip. "Yeah, me too. It was terrible."

It's not like me to open up, but maybe it's the warmth in Rhonda's dark eyes that draws the words out of me. "He was just stuck in the tree . . . and I couldn't get him down . . ."

"I'm so sorry, Flora." Rhonda rubs my arms. "But you're strong. You've been through more than most people."

I know she means well, but I don't feel strong, I feel like my smile is a lie.

"You think so?" I say.

She nods. "I know so. Don't you worry now, I'll make sure we find a solution for Fauna. We'll just need to re-arrange some schedules, but it'll be fine."

Rhonda gives me a reassuring smile and goes over to Fauna. Watching her kneel beside my sister fills my chest with a surge of gratitude.

"Thanks again," I say.

She looks up at me. "My pleasure."

As I make my way across the town square, over the intricate mosaic of light and shadow under the white oak in the center, I wish Carl were with me so I could tell him about the burning in my lightning marks, and the flowers in the grass and in Fauna's room. I pull out my phone.

U okay? I text him.

Suddenly, among the scattered weeds under a linden tree, I spot a lone dandelion, just like the ones in the grass that surrounded Fauna. I don't know why, but I smile at the small flower.

I could swear it lifts its tiny yellow face toward me.

I FEEL MOM'S gaze follow me as we set the table and sit down to our sushi rolls and chopsticks. Then she tries to make casual conversation.

"These are your favorites, right?"

I nod as I savor a bite of California roll. "Thank you," I say swallowing, picking at the lump of green wasabi on my plate with my chopsticks.

"They were out of them," she says, "but the chef made new ones, especially for you."

I give her a smile. "That was nice of him."

We both eat in silence for several minutes, and then Mom puts down her chopsticks. "Do you want to talk about it?" The lines in her forehead deepen. "What happened at that party?"

I knew it. The small talk was just a warmup.

I cram the last sushi roll into my mouth. I don't want to think about the chanting voices, the loud music, the smell of beer, let alone talk about it.

Mom sighs. "Flora, you were half naked in that video. Who did that to you? Was it Jack?"

I continue slowly chewing my sushi roll.

"If you don't tell me, I'll have to speak to the Dunnes about it."

I swallow quickly. "No, don't. Honestly, nothing happened." I stare into the pool of soy sauce on my plate. "It's just that Jack can be such a jerk." I catch myself. "I mean . . . *could* be."

"Oh, honey," Mom says sincerely, "you can talk to me anytime." She places her hand on mine. "About anything."

"I know," I say, painting the soy sauce into daisies with my chopsticks. I haven't told her about Abigail and the flowers, but she's had to deal with enough for one day—for a lifetime, really—so I keep that to myself.

Mom inhales and pushes back her chair, as if she knows she's not going to get anywhere with me tonight. I hear her plate clink against the sink. I get up to rinse mine, but Mom takes the daisy-patterned plate from my hand.

"You must be tired, honey. Let me do the dishes." Her tone tells me she won't listen to protests, which I'm grateful for because I can barely stand up after this terrible day.

"Thanks, Mom." I give her a hug, and she clings to me, holding on a moment longer after I let go.

Before I go upstairs, I glance her way and see her wipe a tear from the corner of her eye.

I HESITATE AT my bedroom door, and instead turn to the one across the hall. I slowly push it open.

Fauna's room is an exact mirror copy of mine. Our rooms were like us, alike but opposites. She was bouncy, loud, wild. Full of singing, laughter, movement. I was the calm one, always capturing moments in my sketchbook, painting still lifes. Now her entire room, her entire existence, is a still life.

My heart aches as I sit on her wrought-iron bed and glance around the room: the drawings I made for her—horses and flowers and landscapes—are taped to the walls, her desk is tidy in a way it never was before the accident, a photo of her smiles as if she's looking right at me.

The summer evening is now fading into shadows. From downstairs I hear Mom's soft voice, the one she uses when she's on the phone with Grandma Christa in Florida. She's telling her about Fauna, telling her and Grandpa Frank not to worry.

I swallow hard, remembering Fauna's strained body, her arched back, her head banging against the headrest, her frantic stuttering. *Noh-noh-noh-noh.* Like she knew what would happen at the party, like she tried to warn me not to go.

"Fauna, don't leave me," I whisper out loud.

I suddenly notice a *tap-tap-tap* coming from my room. I dash across the hall, expecting to see Carl below my window.

But he's not there. Instead, I see a small bird pecking at the glass as if it wants to say something.

Holding my breath, I carefully push the window open so as not to scare the bird away. In the twilight I can see that it's a blue jay. It doesn't flinch, just tilts its head and looks at me with its black bead eyes. Then it pecks twice on the windowsill. When I look closer, I can hardly believe what I see: two acorns, connected by a slender twig.

The bird looks at me briefly, then flaps its wings and disappears into the dark.

Am I dreaming?

I reach for the acorns and it feels surreal, like it's not my hand picking them up, not my fingers twirling the twig between them.

There's a faint tingle in my lightning marks and I am certain I hear Fauna's voice in my head, repeating my words from the day of the lightning.

We're like this . . . you and me.

20

Fauna

Two blue jays sat in a tree.
       One was stung by a bee.
       The other had to flee.
       One blue jay still sits in the tree.

21

FLORA

I BLINK AND SQUINT IN THE BLINDING LIGHT AS THE chatting and chirping of the birds stream in through my open window.

I don't remember falling asleep. I'm still in yesterday's shirt and shorts and the covers are twisted around me. In my closed hand, I feel two small ovals, smooth against my palm.

It wasn't a dream.

I brush the hair out of my face to examine the acorns the blue jay brought me. They're greenish brown, not yet the ripe color of fall.

My phone is still in my back pocket and I pull it out. Nothing from Carl. *Where is he? Why hasn't he answered my message?* I haven't heard from him since he disappeared from the Book Nook yesterday.

> You alright? I type, and then I add:
> We have to meet

Downstairs, I spot a note on the kitchen table.

I didn't want to wake you. You need your rest after yesterday. Take your time and come to the shop when you're ready.
Love, Mom

I check the time on my phone. Already nine o'clock. I grab the orange juice from the fridge and gulp down what's left in the carton. Maybe I can catch Carl at his house before he leaves for camp. That is, if he's still in town.

I KNOCK ON the bright blue door of the Owens', the brass lion knocker roaring a metallic clang with each strike. My hair is still a mess and I weave it quickly between my fingers, leaving a thick braid resting over my shoulder.

Mr. Owen opens the door, wearing his signature striped cardigan and a checkered bowtie. Even during summer break, he looks the part of a history professor. "Hello, Flora." He gives me a hesitant smile, and I can tell I am even more *that girl* to him than before.

From inside the house, Mrs. Owen's shrill voice rings out. "Who is it, Chuck? Is it *The Examiner* again?"

"It's Flora, Phyllis." He sighs as though it's a disappointment that it's just me and not the press corps.

I resist the urge to push Mr. Owen to the side and barge in. Instead I ask, "Is Carl still home?"

"I'm afraid he's not feeling well," Mr. Owen says. "He hasn't been out of his room all morning." He steps aside and lets me into the hallway, which smells faintly of mothballs and wood polish.

Mrs. Owen comes from the kitchen in her green apron, carrying a half-peeled potato. "That was some commotion at your house yesterday!" She says it like an accusation, like we shouldn't have dead boys in our tree in the mornings.

I don't know how to answer. Instead I tug at my wrinkled coral dress that I pulled from the laundry basket just a couple minutes ago. In the silence, I can feel Mrs. Owen's eyes wander over me, and then she leans in close, smelling of fried bacon. "Chin up, we must soldier on."

I force a smile, and she waves the potato peeler at me. "Perhaps you can make him come out."

"Maybe." I hurry up the stairs before she can say anything else.

I knock twice on his closed door. "Hey, Carl? You alright?"

No answer. But there's a muffled sound, then a shuffle across the floor. My heartbeat quickens.

"Come on, it's me." I lean my forehead against the door. "I know you're in there."

A click from the door tells me he unlocked it. I push it open and enter the gloomy cave that is Carl's room. The blinds are down, with only thin stripes of sunlight crawling in through the cracks. With a groan, Carl sinks down onto the floor next to his bed. He rests his head on his arms, cradled by his knees. He doesn't even look up at me.

"Hey." I hesitate for a moment, then sit down next to him. "I thought maybe you skipped town." I chuckle. He glances up at me and I wince as I get a glimpse of his bruised and swollen face.

"I wouldn't leave you, flower-girl," he moans, like it hurts to speak.

I notice his hands match his face; even in the dim light the bruising is obvious. Both sets of knuckles are blue and purple with dried blood painting spider webs in his skin.

I gently pull his left hand to me. "Yesterday it was just your right hand. What happened?"

He yanks it back and turns away from me, but I reach for his shoulder. "You have to tell me."

He flinches at my touch. "They were waiting for me." I don't recognize his voice; the words are barely more than whimpers. "On my way home . . . from Math Wizards."

I can't stand seeing him in such pain. "Who did this to you?"

"Seth . . . and Tyke."

I can feel the rage rise inside; red flashes before my eyes. *Seth and Tyke.* I feel nauseous at the memory of their fingers stroking my skin and their disgusting voices: "Get it off, get it off." And now this. "We have to tell the police," I say. "We have to report them."

He shakes his head slowly. "They know I won't." He's still

turned away from me, like he can't stand me looking at him.

And then I realize. "It's because of Jack, isn't it? Because you're already a suspect."

"Yeah," he grunts.

Gently, I stroke his temple, my fingers caressing his buzz of dark hair. He looks up at me. A cold surge rushes through me, seeing him like this: his cheek blue and swollen, his lip cracked. His eye is puffy and bloodshot and a deep gash across his eyebrow is covered with dry, blackened blood.

"You should see those two clowns . . ." He manages a half smile. "I threw some whopping good punches too."

I smile. "I'm sure you did."

He lets out a chuckle, but then he moans and pulls back, pressing his hand against his side.

Carefully, I put my hand on his shoulder, feeling his every breath rise and fall. "We should get you to a hospital."

"I'll be fine." He shakes me off and awkwardly pulls himself up. "It's just a bruised rib." He eases himself slowly onto the bed, barely moving his stiff upper body.

"Are you kidding me? A bruised rib? How do you know it's not broken?"

He smirks. "I'd know." Then he smiles at me, and there's a glimmer in his eye that I haven't seen before. "This isn't my first rodeo, flower-girl."

Suddenly Carl seems older than his seventeen years, like there might be a completely different person somewhere in there. Like his plain t-shirt and blue jeans are just a disguise, hiding the true Carl I don't really know. He groans again, and I'm pulled out of my brooding.

"Okay, so I'm obviously not going to be able to get you to a hospital. Did you at least get my message?"

His shoulders drop. "No, I didn't see it."

I notice his phone on the nightstand, the screen cracked. "Did Seth and Tyke . . . ?"

He grabs the phone and flings it under the bed where it lands with a *thud*. "Doesn't matter, I don't need it anymore." He pulls another one from his pocket. "I've got a new number, but don't share it with anyone." He texts it to me and I hear the *ping*. I take out my phone to add him to my contacts, but he gently grabs my arm. "Contact me *only* if you really have to."

"Why?"

He shrugs, and I can tell he's trying hard to sound casual. "Lying low, you know." Still, there's that flicker in his good eye. "Can't take any risks."

At first, I wonder what he means, but then I get it. "You think someone tracked your old phone?"

He shrugs and groans again.

I scoot closer to him. "Isn't that kind of paranoid?"

He shoots me a glance, and his silence makes me wonder about the Carl I only get to see glimpses of. The Carl who can pick locks and who can disappear through high windows. The Carl who seems to have learned to fend for himself after years in foster care.

I fumble for the twin acorns in the pocket of my dress. "I wanted to . . ." I hesitate, thinking maybe it's selfish of me to mention something personal with him hurting so much.

"What?" he asks.

"I . . . I wanted to talk to you about something."

He straightens up slightly. "Yeah?"

I pull the acorns from my pocket. "I might be going crazy, but I think I got a message from Fauna."

"What?"

I hand him the acorns and he studies them.

"A blue jay brought them to my window," I say. "Two acorns, like I gave Fauna the day of the accident."

Carl looks at me then back to his hand. "No way. A blue jay?" His eyes return to mine. "You sure?"

I nod. "Last night . . . it tapped on my window and left them on the windowsill."

"A blue jay?" he repeats, carefully handing the acorns back to me.

"I know it sounds weird." I put the treasures back into my pocket and scan Carl's room—at the desk full of schoolbooks, the chair stacked with clothes—as if they could help me explain it. "There's something about the lightning tree. It's like my sister is still there, like I can hear her calling my name."

"Wow," Carl says. Then, seeming to forget about his pain, he says, "We should check it out."

"Right now? Are you sure you can?"

Wincing, he gets up and gently slings his backpack over his shoulders, then turns to me with a smile.

"Anything for you, flower-girl."

22

FAUNA

I couldn't stop it.

Two, this time.

I felt every kick, every last raggedy breath, pulsating through the roots.

"Please, no more," I beg the trees.

But I know this is a mere stretching of limbs, a crackling of knuckles, a warmup before the fight.

23

FLORA

I FOLLOW CARL AS HE SHUFFLES DOWN THE STAIRS, gripping the banister to steady himself.

"Why don't you let me carry your backpack?" I say.

He hushes me and nods to the kitchen, where the Owens' voices carry into the hallway, intermingled with a country song on the radio.

At the bottom of the stairs, I put my arm around his waist and plant his hand on my shoulder, giving him a stern look that says, *Don't you dare push me away.* He lets out a muffled moan, then winks at me.

We hobble across the hallway, careful not to catch the Owens' attention. I pull the blue door open, but as we cross the threshold, Mrs. Owen says, "And what are you two up to?"

We both stop at the same time. Our backs still turned to her, I force a cheerful tone. "Just going out."

"Caaaarl?" Mrs. Owen says, stretching out his name like a rubber band with a snap at the end.

He exhales and we slowly turn around.

Mrs. Owen gasps. "My goodness, what happened to you?"

"Just . . . messing around with a couple of kids at camp." Carl shifts his weight and straightens up. "I didn't want to worry you, so I—"

"Worry me?" Mrs. Owen's face turns red. She smooths her green apron in sharp strokes like exclamation marks as she speaks. "First the police come looking for you, and now this." Her already shrill voice rises. "I honestly don't know what to do with you." She turns to the kitchen. "Chuck, come out here. Look what he got himself into this time."

Carl lets out a sigh, then abruptly turns around and drags me out the door. Behind us we hear Mrs. Owen squeal, "You come back here, Carl Nielsen! There's a murderer on the loose!"

But Carl doesn't look back as he scurries beside me across the front yard.

AS WE FOLLOW Pine Ridge Road back to my house, Carl isn't leaning against me anymore, and I miss the weight of his arm over my shoulders.

"Hey, did that police officer find you?" I ask.

"Chief Batista?" Carl nods. "He showed up at Math Wizards yesterday, but Aaron covered for me. Told him I was home sick."

We turn at the hawthorn hedge and come up the driveway. I bite my lip and stop. I've been avoiding looking at the oak tree, but now I have no choice.

The grass underneath is still littered with bits of police tape, scattered among cut-off twigs and branches. But the beer cans are all gone, as are the gasoline can and the axe, presumably collected as evidence. There's a hole in the tree's crown, like the firefighters brought part of the tree down with Jack. A few strings of frayed toilet paper are still swaying in the breeze. Other than that, there are no signs of the terrible events that took place yesterday. It seems unreal that only a day ago, Jack was up there, lifeless, staring down at Mom and me with unseeing eyes.

A shudder runs through me. I draw a deep breath and walk up to the tree.

"I don't get it." Carl follows me closely, pressing his hand to his side. "You heard your sister? How's that even possible?"

"I don't know." I reach for the trunk and feel the familiar tingling in my lightning marks travel across the back of my hand and up my arm. "You better stand back," I tell Carl.

"What? I come all this way with you, and now you tell me to go away?" Carl teases. He rolls his eyes and sits stiffly onto the grass, about ten feet from the tree.

"I think that maybe . . ." I place both my palms against the trunk, feeling the furrows in the bark. The tree's scar is still as wide as the day the lightning struck, only softer, less raw, at the edges.

The tingling in my skin increases. It's not my imagination. I can feel it clearly, like a faint electric pulse running from the tree and into the palms of my hands, my arms, my chest, my heart. It's like a humming, a song, a melody that I didn't know I missed. I close my eyes and press my arms against the trunk, my cheek to the rough bark.

I can feel the melody grow, burning in my lightning marks, just like when I climbed the tree after we found Jack. A strong current moves up and down my arms, and spreads into my neck, my chest. I can barely breathe as it consumes me. And there it is again: my name, over and over.

Flora, Flora, Flora, Flora, Flora.

Fauna's voice, in my skin, in the tree, in my flesh and bones. It's like the lightning again, burning through me, like I'm falling, falling. *Forgive me, Fauna, I should have protected you. I should have caught you, never let you fall. Forgive me, forgive me—*

"Flora."

I open my eyes and see Carl looking at me with concern. *Where am I?* I suddenly realize I'm on the ground, with my head resting in Carl's lap.

"You okay?" he asks, brushing a strand of hair from my cheek. Above him, the crown of the oak tree slowly billows in the breeze, the blue sky peeking through.

I smile. *Fauna. She is here.* I can still feel that faint tingling in my skin, like an echo of her voice.

"I had to drag you from the tree," Carl says. "You were clinging to it and calling for your sister."

"I was?"

"Yeah. What happened?"

I squint as the green of the treetop and the blue of the sky melt into a blur and begin to spin. I blink hard and shift my focus to Carl's eyes, to that golden speck in his left iris that I haven't noticed before. "It was . . . I can't describe it."

"Try." Even through the swelling, his eyes have that softness he only has when he looks at me.

"It was like we talked, Fauna and I . . . or like we shared each other's thoughts." I sit up, but the vertigo forces me to press my forehead to my knees.

"You sure you're okay?" Carl asks.

Before I can respond, we hear footsteps crunching in the gravel. I look up and see Aaron running toward us.

Panting, he stops and bends over, his hands on his knees. "You need . . . to come . . ." He gestures toward the street.

There's a sudden knot in my stomach. "What is it?"

"Just come with me." Aaron sucks in air through his teeth, then gives Carl a double-take. "Man, you get hit by a car?"

"Something like that." Carl stands with a grimace.

"Well, you have to see this," Aaron insists.

We follow Aaron along the road toward the forest. He leads us up the narrow trail into the woods, to the shortcut to Derwyn Middle School. "Come on, guys," he shouts over his shoulder. Beams of sunlight fall between the trees, and the air is full of drifting pollen, like clouds of golden dust.

But something is wrong.

It's the silence. No birds are chirping. There's only the smell of moss and dry leaves rising from the ground.

"I was on my way to Math Wizards," Aaron says. "I didn't know what to do."

The knot in my stomach tightens. Aaron's panic-stricken voice reminds me of Mom that morning we found Jack.

He continues to lead us along the trail, the soft strokes of ferns brushing against my calves with every step.

"This is where they were waiting for me," Carl says under his breath.

"Who? Seth and Tyke?" I whisper back.

He nods and stops. I hear Aaron groan.

I look up.

There they are. Both of them. High above us, trapped in a birch tree like two giant flies.

"Oh, my God," I utter. My knees fail me, and I sink to the ground.

Their faces are full of scratches, just like Jack.

The branches of the tree are curled around their necks, their chests, their shoulders, just like Jack.

Seth and Tyke . . . they are both blue and lifeless, just like Jack.

24

FAUNA

A new cry echoes through the forest.

From tree to tree, shooting through the roots, the branches, the trembling leaves.

A battle cry.

25

FLORA

Seth's and Tyke's eyes look down on us, fixed and unblinking.

They are too high up to reach.

I press my arms to my stomach to quench the nausea. I don't want to look at them, but I have to. Their limp bodies are entangled in a web of branches, their faces full of scratches, like they've been attacked by wild animals. I can distinguish the jagged lines of a crooked X on both of their foreheads, the blood already dry and dark. I barely recognize them, but there is no doubt: Tyke's silver ring glimmers on his hand among the leaves, and Seth's thin moustache is visible above his gaping mouth, frozen in a silent scream.

"They must have been here since yesterday," Carl says.

"You mean . . . up in the tree?" Aaron inhales deeply. "Who could have done this? A second time?"

I pull myself to my feet, my knees shaking. "I think I'm gonna be sick." The octopus is back again, pulling its tentacles through my stomach. I have to bend into the underbrush and let it all out. I am cold and shivering one minute, then hot and sticky the next.

I feel Carl's hand on my back. "You alright?"

Swiping my hair from my face, I straighten up and whisper, "Yeah. I just can't believe it happened again. Who could do such a terrible thing?"

Carl doesn't say anything, just takes shallow breaths with his hand pressed against his ribs.

Out of the corner of my eye, I can see Aaron drawing closer to the bodies, studying them. The bruising on their scratched faces is obvious. It's not as much as Carl's, but Seth has a black eye, and Tyke has a purple lesion on his chin.

Aaron turns to Carl. "Hit by a car, huh?" His gaze lingers on the pointed gash above Carl's eyebrow, the imprint of half a star—the shape of Tyke's ring.

Carl staggers over to Aaron. "They were waiting for me after Math Wizards. They could've killed me!"

Aaron takes a step back. "So, you . . ." He glances toward the bodies in the tree, shaking his head.

"No!" Carl cringes.

"He didn't do it!" I struggle to keep my voice steady. "I mean how could he have . . .?"

Aaron shifts his weight. "You just beat them up a little, is that what you're saying?"

"They started it! I had to defend myself!" Carl can't talk without wincing, but continues. "I would never do anything like this! How could you even think that?"

"I don't know what to think." Aaron's exhale sounds like a moan. He surveys the bodies, their surreal positions in the tree. "This is insane. It's almost like the tree grabbed them from the ground."

"What do we do?" Carl is hugging himself like he's freezing and I can hear the pain in his voice.

"We should call the police." Aaron pulls his phone from his pocket.

I reach for him. "We can't."

"But we can't just leave them like this." His voice breaks, and I realize what it must be like for Aaron, seeing his friends like this, guys he's known since kindergarten.

"Okay," I concede, "I guess you can. But Carl and I can't be here when they come. It would be too suspicious. We're already persons of interest, or whatever they call it."

Aaron hesitates, weighing the phone in his hand. "What will you do then?"

I look at Carl. "We need to lie low for a while, at least Carl—"

Aaron suddenly motions for us to be quiet. Voices from farther down the trail echo our way, probably kids on their way to summer camp at the middle school. Someone laughs, the light voice bouncing between the trees, and my heart aches. They're just kids; they shouldn't see this.

Carl is tugging at my arm. "Flora, come on."

The voices are coming closer. They'll be here any second.

I nod a goodbye to Aaron and lead Carl off the trail and

into the underbrush of the forest, running through ferns and shrubs that bite my bare legs. Behind us I hear Aaron telling the kids to turn back.

We are farther into the woods now, jumping over fallen tree trunks, slipping on moss-covered stones, ducking under sprigs. We could stop, could take it slower, but soon this whole part of the woods will be full of policemen, firefighters, paramedics—just like my front yard yesterday. *Was it really only yesterday?*

I feel my lightning marks burn and pulsate with each heartbeat. My hands find the peeling trunk of a birch tree, then the smooth bark of a young maple. I hear whispering and call out to Carl behind me as I run. "What did you say?"

"Nothing," Carl says. Then, "Ouch! These damn twigs."

But I was sure I heard someone whisper, *cut, cut, cut.* One voice, or several voices melting together around me.

When I glance back, I see Carl stumbling, holding his hands to his side, groaning and gasping for air. I notice a few scratches on his face too. I realize that I've known these woods since I was a child, but Carl has no idea how far we have left to go. "We'll be at my place soon," I tell him. "Just a little bit farther."

When we finally arrive at the meadow behind my house, I motion for Carl to stop. Crouching behind a fallen tree trunk, I scan our house and yard. Carl sinks down, his back to the trunk. All is still, just a breeze caressing the tall grass and the trembling crown of our oak.

"All clear," I tell Carl over my shoulder.

As we run through the meadow, I hear Carl's labored breathing behind me. By the time we reach the porch, he is bent over with pain, his arms wrapped around him. I unlock the door and help him into our kitchen.

"Here, sit down." I pull out a chair, grab a glass from the cabinet, and fill it with water. As I set it on the table in front of him, the last of my strength leaves me, my knees, my feet, my lungs. I sink down onto the chair next to him.

My vision blurs and everything fades into darkness, everything except for Carl's beautiful, bruised face, his brown eyes.

He catches me staring at him in horror. "What?" he gasps.

I reach out and caress the smooth skin at his hairline with my thumb. I don't know how to tell him that the scratches on his forehead bleed together into a crooked, but distinct, X.

26

F A U N A

"All this violence," the trees cry.

"A single act of violence can destroy what took years, decades, centuries, to grow. Moment after painstaking moment of nurture and protection.

An act of violence and it's gone.

The violent always win.

Hard against soft, steel against flesh.

The soft must bend and break and be crushed.

But not anymore."

27

FLORA

"CARL, YOU . . ." MY VOICE TREMBLES.

He touches his forehead, his eyes widening. "My God, Flora. Is it . . . ?"

I nod, my hand over my mouth.

He gets up. "I need to see it."

I support him across the kitchen and up the stairs. In my room, we both stop cold in front of the mirror. Our horrified faces stare back at us. The scratches in Carl's forehead are deep and crooked, meeting in an eerily centered bloody X.

"Hold on," I say.

I dampen a towel in the bathroom, and when I return, Carl is sitting on my bed.

"Here," I offer, tenderly dabbing his forehead.

"Ouch!" Carl winces. "It must have happened when we ran through the woods, some whopping twigs or branches."

"Sit still," I admonish when he pulls back. As I wipe, the X becomes even more obvious, and I shudder. "I know how this is going to sound but . . . Seth and Tyke had the same kind of cuts." I gently press the towel against his forehead. "And Jack."

Carl nods slightly. "But Seth and Tyke already had them when they attacked me, as if they'd been marked somehow."

"Did they say how they got them? The X's?" I peek under the towel, but the scratches are still bleeding and I press the towel back to his forehead.

Carl shakes his head. "It wasn't like I got a chance to ask them about it before they started swinging at me. They kept saying it was my fault Jack was dead."

I catch him surveying my room, as if he's looking for escape routes. I lift the white towel, now patterned with red and pink blotches. "There, it's not bleeding anymore."

I go into the bathroom to rinse the towel. As I watch Carl's blood swirl down the drain, I remember how he disappeared from the Book Nook and wonder if he'll still be in my room when I get back.

Luckily, he hasn't moved. Only now he's staring off into the distance in a way that strangely reminds me of Fauna. He looks up at me and motions to his forehead. "All four of us, the same mark. There must be some connection. Something we're missing."

A shiver runs through me. While we ran home, I know I heard the words *cut, cut, cut* all around me, like they came from the forest itself.

"The trees," I say. "Do you think they did this? All of it?"

I close my eyes, remembering. "It was like . . . I could hear them in my skin." I open my eyes and look at the faded zigzags on my arms. "Right before they cut you."

Carl is silent for several moments, then says, "No. We have to think about it rationally." He holds up three fingers. "Three people, dead in the same way. No leads, except for the X's in their foreheads and the way they were found, entangled in trees." He speaks matter-of-factly, like he's working on a lab report.

I drag the wicker chair from my desk and sit opposite him. "And two different locations, at least two miles apart."

"Right," Carl says, "which indicates this wasn't a random act of violence, but more of a coordinated attack."

"As if the trees were self-aware, and . . ." I search for the right word. ". . . mobilized."

Carl pulls a face. "It's more likely a crazy coincidence, don't you think? I mean, trees attacking humans . . ." His voice fades and I can tell we're both thinking the same thing. *Or a psychopath, a serial killer.*

I shake my head in quick bursts, trying to push the frightening thoughts away. "And why Jack, Seth, and Tyke? Why those marks?" I don't say: *The same as you have.*

"I don't know. Nothing seems to make sense. And how did they manage to do it?"

"They," I echo.

"Yeah, *they*. The trees." His look of horror matches mine.

"It's insane," I say.

Carl nods. "Completely, whopping insane."

I take in a breath and can't help but cringe inside at the X on Carl's forehead. And then, out of nowhere, I remember something I stumbled across when I researched my science presentation on climate change.

"Wait . . . if we're working from the hypothesis that it really could be the trees that are behind the killings, they must have—" I grab my laptop and plop down on the bed next to Carl. "—communicated with each other."

I type *trees* and *communicate* in the search field, then press enter. There are a ton of hits. Articles, books, videos. But the one that stands out is an article titled, "How Trees Communicate Through Their Roots," written by a German scientist.

I scan the article, feeling a surge of adrenaline. "It says here that they talk through an intricate web of fungus, that it's an electrochemical communication going on between the roots."

Carl leans in and continues reading over my shoulder. "Trees are avid conversationalists, speaking in the language of carbon, nitrogen, phosphorus, water, and hormones. If they are attacked by, for example, bugs, they send warning signals to other trees. They also feel pain and experience loss when a neighboring tree dies. One study has even found that plants and trees emit an ultrasonic 'scream' when in pain, such as from cuts or drought." I feel his breath on my neck as he says, "Can you believe that? Trees actually feel pain. And they can warn each other about danger."

"It's incredible," I say. "And look at this." I point to the screen. "Trees can talk with each other from a great distance, thanks to their extensive underground communication system."

"Whoa. Who knew?"

"Trees have families and friends," I continue, "and they nurture their children, sending nutrients through the roots. Old mother trees function as hubs, creating highways in this busy underground network."

We look at each other in awe. Then Carl's eyes grow large. "Oh man . . . I just thought of something." He grabs his phone from his pocket, types in *trees marked for cutting,* and clicks on "images." He scrolls through the pictures and I gasp. Every image shows trees with X's painted in blue, orange, white, or red on their trunks.

"They're doing it to *us* now," he says. "They're eliminating us, like we do them." He touches his forehead. "This must mean I'm next."

We're staring at each other in disbelief when I'm startled by a text from Mom.

Are you okay?

I glance at Carl, glued to the images on his phone.

I'm not feeling well, I think I'd
better stay home from the shop
today. Is that okay?

She texts back immediately.

That's fine, honey. You rest.
Call me if you need anything.

Thanks, Mom, I type.

"Everything okay?" Carl asks.

"Yeah. It was just Mom, checking on me."

"She's cool with you staying home?"

"She said she was."

"Good," he says absentmindedly, scrolling on his phone.

The investigating seems to be taking Carl's mind off his pain, and I'm glad. But all this stuff has really made me miss the one person I know could help us.

"It's just . . ." I start.

He looks up. "Just what?"

"I was just thinking . . . how I wish my dad were here."

Carl nods. "Oh right . . . he was a botanist. He gave you and Fauna your names."

"Yeah, and I'm sure he'd be able to tell us more." I look out the window to the oak tree, which my dad used to tend to as if it was his own child.

"So you don't know where he is, huh?"

I shake my head. "No idea."

"Name?" Carl asks, poised to type it into my laptop.

I sigh. "I've already googled him like a billion times."

"And?" Carl raises his eyebrows with a moan as his bruised skin strains around the scratches in his forehead.

"Nothing but old references. Articles he wrote."

"Come on, there must be something more recent. What's his first name?"

"Seriously, you won't find anything. I don't even know if he's dead or alive. We haven't heard from him since he left us when I was ten."

"You haven't tried my magic touch." He flashes his dimpled smile, slowly this time, like the Cheshire Cat.

"Okay, okay," I concede, unable to resist his smile. "It's David."

"What college did he go to? He had a title, right?"

I mentally scan my faded memories, conversations I didn't think much of at the time. "He got a PhD from the University of Philadelphia."

Carl taps the keypad and searches. "Let's see," he murmurs. "Here are those old articles you mentioned, ones on moss and photosynthesis that he wrote."

"Yeah, but after that . . . it's like he just disappeared."

"Wait!" Carl says. "Check this out."

On the screen there's a video titled "David Reed, PhD, NI Lecture." I inhale sharply and point to the date below it. "It was uploaded yesterday?"

We look at each other, then back at the frozen image on

the screen. The camera is positioned low, like it's on a desk in a classroom, angled toward a whiteboard. A man stands in front of it, wearing a white lab coat over a plaid shirt and baggy blue jeans. He is paler and thinner than I remember, but his unkempt hair has that wave of blond, now graying, that Mom says I inherited.

"Oh my gosh, that's him," I blurt out.

Carl clicks play. My dad's voice is agitated, like he's conveying a critical life-or-death message. "We have focused on extraterrestrial life and artificial intelligence when we should have looked to what is already among us."

It's him. It's really him. I recognize that deep, raspy voice from the childhood memories I have played over and over in my head, all the times he pointed out the names of trees and weeds and flowers to Fauna and me, his face in the crack of my door, smiling as he said good night.

"We have long known that nature is sentient to some degree," he continues. "That natural beings such as plants and trees can sense their surroundings and feel pain, even be on alert for enemies, but we haven't known to what degree they are self-aware, mainly because of the communication barrier, meaning they've had no effective way to communicate their feelings and thoughts, if you will, to humans. But when it happens it will . . ." He turns with excitement to the whiteboard. A bright flare makes it difficult to see what he's writing, and with his voice projected toward the board, we only hear muffled mumbling.

Then he turns back to the camera again. "It is evolution, plain and simple. The next step." He makes a sweeping motion with his hands. "And when it happens it will be a revolution. The Natural Intelligence Revolution." He pronounces each word slowly, then underlines those same words on the whiteboard.

The Natural Intelligence Revolution.

My dad comes closer to the camera, leans over, and the video ends.

I realize I've been holding my breath and finally exhale. "Do you think he was talking about *this*?" I look at the crooked X scratched into Carl's forehead. "Play it again."

Carl taps the button.

"We have focused on—"

"Wait." I nudge Carl.

The picture freezes and I point to the corner of the whiteboard. "There's some sort of symbol."

Carl squints and leans closer to the screen. "It looks like the logo of a company that makes weed killer."

I grab my phone and take a picture of the screen, zooming in on the symbol. "What do you think it means?"

We both examine the black-and-white, diamond-shaped logo. It's sharp at the edges, giving it an ominous look, and in the middle, there's the image of a seed, cracked open with a sprout growing out of it, carrying a single leaf.

28

FAUNA

The marks.
X for cut.
A warning, a countdown, a death sentence.
The one word that humans taught the trees.

29

FLORA

A SERIES OF POUNDINGS ON THE FRONT DOOR ECHOES through the house.

I look at Carl. "Who can that be?"

His bruised eyes narrow. "Maybe Aaron?"

I get up from the bed. "Stay here. And stay quiet."

"Yes, ma'am," he mocks.

Through the glass in the front door, I see it's Chief Batista. Before I can dodge his view, he spots me and waves hello like we're friends.

I open the door. "Mom isn't here," I say. "And she doesn't want me to talk to you without her."

"I know, but . . ." He clears his throat. "I really need to ask you a few more questions. Is anyone else here, your dad perhaps?" He looks over my shoulder and into the house.

"He left a long time ago." I realize this isn't very clear. "Like, when I was a kid," I add.

"Oh, I see." Chief Batista frowns. "Your mom didn't mention that."

I cross my arms over my chest.

He clears his throat again. "Miss Reed, I'm sorry to say that there have been two more . . ." He hesitates. ". . . tree-jackings."

"Tree-jackings?"

"Yes. That's apparently what people are calling them now. After Jack, I presume." He shifts his weight in his black police boots. "Two more boys have been found . . ." He hesitates again. ". . . dead."

I close my eyes, haunted by the image of Seth and Tyke in the birch tree. To hear it from Chief Batista somehow makes it more real, but I can't let him suspect that I already know.

"That's terrible," I say sincerely. "Who were they?"

"Seth Moore and Thomas—'Tyke'—O'Reilly. Did you know them?"

"Not really. I mean, we went to the same school, but we barely talked."

Chief Batista grabs the notepad from his chest pocket. "Is it all right if I . . . ?" He motions to the wicker sofa on our porch.

"Sure, go ahead."

He sits down on the faded indigo cushion, and I sit on the edge of the swing, clasping the rusty chains.

Chief Batista looks at me with a frown. "Miss Reed, I spoke with Seth and Tyke the day that you and your mom found Jack."

His gaze wanders to the scarred oak tree. Everything is quiet except for the birds singing, the cicadas buzzing, and a light breeze whispering in the hawthorn hedge. The thought of Carl so close to Chief Batista makes my heart race and my hands clammy. I have to get rid of the chief as soon as possible without him being suspicious.

"They told me what happened that night after the party." He sighs and flips open his notepad. "Apparently, they became quite drunk at the party. But you already knew that."

I can feel the edge of the swing dig into my bare legs.

"Sometime around midnight, Jack decided he needed to restore his honor, apparently by TP-ing your house." He smirks. "They took Seth's car and drove over here, all three of them, drunk as sailors, and started to, uh, well . . ." He nods to the oak tree.

I shift my legs slightly and the chain creaks. I move my hands to my lap, conscious not to fiddle too much.

"According to Seth, Jack was so angry, he wanted to cut the tree down and found an axe in the trunk of the car. It was dark, but Tyke recalled hearing Jack swearing like a madman while attacking the tree, too drunk to inflict more than a few scrapes." Chief Batista leans in closer. "But here's where it gets really interesting." He taps his forehead. "They were both scratched when I talked to them, marked with X's like Jack. And when I asked them about it, they said it was the tree."

He waits for my reaction, and I remember I have to act surprised. "That's really weird," I say, trying to sound genuine.

"Weird is right. They both admitted to being intoxicated that night, but still maintained it was the tree that cut them. In Tyke's words: 'Like it came alive or something.'"

I draw a deep breath, but the chief is looking at his scribblings and doesn't notice.

"Apparently, Jack got so furious, he ran back to the car, got the can of gasoline, and shouted, 'Burn in hell, stupid tree.'"

He pauses to study me as Tyke's words echo in my mind: *Like it came alive or something.* I remember the pungent stench of gasoline that morning. "That explains—" I stop myself from saying, *Why the tree needed to defend itself.* Instead I mutter, "All the stuff we found on the ground."

Chief Batista nods. "Seth said he'd never seen Jack that angry. Like he was possessed, running around pouring gasoline on a tree in the dark." He reads again from the notepad. "Seth and Tyke confessed to helping Jack at this point, passing the gas can between them, while trying to, and I quote, 'fend off the tree.'" The words give him pause. "Then all of a sudden, Jack became quiet. Seth and Tyke searched for him, but when they couldn't find him, they panicked and fled the scene." Batista leans back. "And now those two boys are dead. The only two witnesses."

I'm not sure what to say, but luckily, Chief Batista cuts

the momentary silence. "The question is, how did Jack end up in the tree?"

I shrug. "I have no idea."

"But I think you do. I think you know much more than you're letting on."

I shake my head innocently. "I don't."

It's like Batista's eyes are holding mine hostage and I can't look away. But there's nothing I can tell him. What? That I suspect the trees? That I read on the internet that trees can feel pain and talk to each other? That I heard them whisper as I ran through the woods? That would sound insane, even coming from *that girl*.

Chief Batista shifts his weight, making the sofa squeak. "Please, I need you to tell me anything you know, no matter how small or unimportant you think it might be. Right now, we're treating this as the work of a serial killer."

My heart beats so fast I worry the chief might see it pulsing under the thin cotton of my dress. "You are?"

"Yes. So you can understand why we're eager to talk to anyone who might give us insight into the case."

I nod and look down at my hands, so tightly balled into fists that my knuckles are white.

"Miss Reed, do you know where Carl Nielsen might be? We haven't been able to locate him."

I swallow and shake my head. There's no way Chief Batista can see the wounds in Carl's forehead and his bruised face, tying him to Seth and Tyke.

"He lives right next door to you, Miss Reed," the chief prods. "Isn't it possible that he heard them in your yard, came over to confront Jack, and they started fighting again? That things got out of hand and he finished the job?"

"But I'm sure he didn't . . . he wouldn't . . ." I stammer.

Chief Batista leans in close again, close enough that I can see a few gray strands in his dark stubble and smell his musky scent. "He might be dangerous, Miss Reed. If you know anything, you need to tell me."

Footsteps approach in the gravel, and I recognize the female police officer, from the morning we found Jack, coming up the driveway.

"Chief, the search warrant came through." She holds up her phone, showing some sort of electronic document. "Signed and clear."

"Thanks, Officer Herrera." Chief Batista closes his notepad with a single flip. "I'm sorry, Miss Reed. We'll need to search your home now."

My stomach tightens. "Don't you need to ask my mom's permission?"

Chief Batista shakes his head. "'Fraid not."

All I can think about is Carl upstairs in my room. He can't be arrested; he didn't do it. And I need him. I get up from the swing and back away from Chief Batista toward the door.

"Just let me clean my room a bit. It's a total mess."

They both squint at me and I know they don't buy it.

"Like embarrassingly messy," I add in a perfect girly teenager voice.

Without waiting for an answer, I rush inside and up the stairs. I hear them come into the foyer. "We'll give you a minute and then we're coming up," Batista shouts.

I don't have any time to text Mom. I have barely enough time to get Carl out of the house. I find him standing by the open window, his backpack over his shoulders, holding a thin, black rope that loops around my bedpost and is coiled around his waist, like a mountain climber.

I close my door quietly. "What are you doing?" I whisper. "Where did you get—"

He's already halfway out the window. "Let's meet at Aaron's place. You know where he lives?"

"I'll find it."

Carl steps over the sill, clenching the rope.

"But your rib," I say.

He winks at me. "I'll be alright."

"Wait," I urge him. I dash to my closet and grab my red Phillies cap. "Here." I slap it on his head, and he pulls it down over his forehead with a muffled groan.

"Go!" I whisper.

He grunts as he leans back and starts rappelling to the ground. I brace myself against the bed as his weight tugs on it. He lands and pulls the rope over the windowsill just as I hear boots on the stairs.

"Miss Reed? We're coming in." Chief Batista opens the

door and stops in the doorway, with Officer Herrera right behind him. Their eyes scan my messy room.

"You weren't kidding." He smiles. "I bet your mom gives you a hard time about this. I know I would."

I glance at my laptop, still open. *I can't let them see my latest searches.* Glaring at Chief Batista, I say, "What are you, my dad?"

His smile fades. Officer Herrera makes a sweep of the bathroom, and I hold my breath. *The bloody towel in the sink. Did I get most of it out?* I wonder.

"All clear," she says. I exhale slowly and discreetly close my laptop.

"We need to take a look around the rest of the house too," the chief says.

"Fine," I tell him.

I follow them through the upstairs, then the downstairs. Satisfied that I'm not harboring a fugitive, they make their way out the front door and down our driveway.

As soon as they're out of sight, I run upstairs and reopen my laptop. The image of my dad is still frozen in the frame of the video: his messy hair, his raised arms like wings in the lab coat. Then I notice there are a couple of messages in the comments section under the video.

"Is this a joke?!"

"What a lunatic."

It figures people don't believe it.

For so long, I've wished I had a way to reach my dad,

and this is my chance. I hesitate, though, my fingers stiff over the keyboard. There's so much I want to say, so much that I want to ask him. But I can't ask, *Why did you leave us? Why haven't you been in touch?* And typing *Could trees kill people?* feels insane.

With my heart pounding, I instead type: *Where are you, Dad? I need you.*

I press enter and watch my comment appear under the others. I feel like I'm throwing a message in a bottle into the sea. But maybe he'll read it. And maybe he'll reach out to me and finally give me some answers—to more questions than one.

30

FAUNA

It is set in motion, and there's no going back.

A loose stone must roll down the hill. A seed in the soil must break open. A bird pushed out of her nest must spread her wings. A caterpillar must become a chrysalis and then a butterfly. A tree must learn to fight.

Motion, growth, change is the law of survival.

31

FLORA

I RING THE DOORBELL BELOW THE OVAL BRASS PLAQUE that reads BLUMENFELD. Only a few seconds pass before Aaron opens the door and pulls me inside.

"Did anyone see you?" He swiftly locks the door behind me.

"I don't think so. Why?"

Aaron pushes his hands into the pockets of his jeans. "Just being cautious, I guess." He avoids looking at me, but I can see that his eyes are red and a little swollen.

I reach out and touch his arm. "You alright?" I can feel him tremble through the soft fabric of his shirt.

He stiffens and shakes his head, trying to keep his emotion in check. "How do you do it, Flora?"

"What?"

"Go on with your life."

I shrug. "I don't know. You just have to, I guess."

I know it sounds lame, but it's the truth. When your dad disappears, when your sister gets struck by lightning, when you find dead schoolmates in trees, you still go on living, even though a part of you feels like your life has been pushed off the road you were supposed to be on.

I can tell that Aaron feels untethered the way I do right now as he wipes his eyes with the back of his hand. I wish I had a brilliant explanation for how I'm going on after what's happened, but I don't.

He nods and says, "Well, thanks for coming." His voice breaks.

I wrap him in a hug. "It'll get better," I whisper. His arms tighten around me, like he hasn't been held in a long time. As we cling to each other, we sway back and forth a little, and somehow it isn't awkward.

"Flora?"

Carl appears on the stairs.

Aaron and I untangle from each other in a millisecond. I smooth my dress, and Aaron pulls his hand through his thick, brown hair, both of us acting like we've just been caught making out or something.

Carl's still wearing the Phillies cap. "I was worried about you." He takes my hand and pulls me into the hallway. For an instant I worry that he's upset finding me hugging Aaron, but instead he says, "I can't believe they searched your house."

"Oh. Yeah, I know. They didn't stay long, though. They just went through every room looking for you." I stop and exchange a conspiratorial smirk with Carl. "And then they left." I'm amazed at how natural my hand feels in Carl's. "I can't believe you climbed out my window like a total pro."

He shrugs like it was no big deal, then squeezes my hand as if to say *I've got you. Everything will be alright.*

We find Aaron in the living room. Carl lets go of my hand and I instantly miss him, miss being *gotten*. But that is quickly eclipsed by how empty Aaron's living room feels. Even though there are modern angular sofas, side tables, and lamps, there is nothing personal, not even any photos.

"Did I hear someone say that your dad works in Europe?" I ask him.

Aaron nods. "Yeah. in London. He's a stockbroker."

"What about your mom?"

"She's a cardiologist. She got a job six months ago in New York City. She comes home as much as she can, but she's really swamped this week."

"So you basically live here alone?"

Aaron gives a nonchalant shrug, like not having his parents around is no big deal. But now I understand why he seemed starved for a hug.

"Have you at least talked to your Mom?" I ask. "About what happened?"

"Not yet," he says, then deflects to me. "What about you? Is your mom all freaked out?"

"She's managing, I guess."

I want to say, *I don't think any of us know what to think, especially about trees killing people,* but no one knows anything about that yet besides Carl and me.

I grab the back of the black leather sofa as images of bodies in trees run through my mind, giving me a surge of nausea.

"Flora, you okay?" Carl wraps his arm around my waist and I press my face against his shoulder. His t-shirt smells like a summer day. He guides me to a chair and I sink down.

"I'm okay, just a little lightheaded." I rest my arms on the table and trace the lines in the wood, the swirls and tiny cracks. There's a faint tingle in my skin, and I become acutely aware of the sacrifice the tree made to become this piece of furniture, almost as if it is whispering to me.

Aaron puts a glass of water in front of me, and I gulp it down. Coldness spreads in my chest and chases the nausea away.

"I'm fine. It's just . . . it's been . . ." I feel like I'm fumbling beyond the limits of language, pulling back an empty hand every time I try to form a sentence.

Seeming to understand me without words, Aaron says, "Yeah. I've been talking to police and paramedics all day. Have they been questioning you too?"

I nod. "Yeah, I mean, they even searched my house."

"Carl told me . . . how they were looking for him."

I nod again.

Aaron's eyes dart between Carl and me. "Guys. Seriously. What's happening? Who do you think's doing this?"

Carl and I exchange looks, silently saying, *We have to tell him about our theory, no matter how outlandish it sounds.*

I inhale. "Well . . . we think . . ." I bite my lip. ". . . it might be the trees."

Aaron's brow furrows. "Are you kidding?" He lets out a laugh, then scoffs, "You *are* kidding, right?"

Carl squirms in his chair. "Actually, no. Flora has . . . some kind of connection to them."

Aaron looks at me and then back at Carl. "You guys can't be serious!"

I sigh. "I know it sounds completely nuts, but it's like I can hear them . . . or *feel* them. Like there's this secret language, waiting to be deciphered or something." I trace the faded lightning marks on my wrist. "Like the words are there, only just out of reach."

Before Aaron can mock me, an idea crosses my mind.

"But wait . . . what if . . ."

Carl leans forward. "What?"

"If I could bring Fauna to the oak tree."

"What would bringing Fauna there do?"

"It's hard to explain," I say, "but I think it could be our answer."

"How?" Aaron wants to know, still skeptical.

"Well, it's as if there's a piece of her still in the tree, and if we bring her to it, I might be able to connect with her. Or with the tree. Or both." Excitement pulses through me. "Maybe I can talk to her, ask her why the trees are doing this."

Aaron stares at us wide-eyed. "Your sister? I thought she didn't speak?"

"She doesn't." I hesitate. "Well, not with words. But she speaks to me in other ways. In flowers. In acorns."

I shoot Carl a *please help me* look.

"It's not as crazy as it sounds," Carl says.

Aaron snorts. "It couldn't sound any crazier."

"Here." Carl pulls out his phone. "Read this."

Aaron reads the title of the German scientist's article out loud, then gives us a cynical look.

"Just read it," Carl urges.

While Aaron digests the article, Carl leans closer and takes my hand. "Will they let you bring Fauna home, just like that?"

"I don't know."

The warmth of Carl's hand is like fire warming my entire body. He rubs the back of my hand with his thumb and shivers shoot up my arm. *Like the trees*, I think. *The way my lightning scars tingle and burn when I touch them, or am even close to them.* It is similar to Carl's touch, yet completely different—like two different languages, or like the difference between spoken words and sign language.

"Do you have any ideas?" Carl wants to know.

"Not yet. But I'll think of something."

"I'm sure you will." Carl winks.

"Okay." Aaron plunks the phone down on the table. "I get it. Trees talk."

"*And* they warn each other of danger." Carl lets go of my hand and pulls off the Phillies cap. "And they attack."

Aaron sees the scratched X, dried and crooked, for the first time and his face turns gray. "Oh, man. Does that mean you're . . . *next*?"

Carl gingerly puts the cap back on. "Believe me, that's what I've been wondering. But why Seth and Tyke? And why me?"

"Chief Batista told me that all three of them—Jack, Seth and Tyke—tried to harm our oak tree the night of the party. They all got marked. But only Jack died that night."

"But the trees got to them later anyway," Aaron says.

"But why me?" Carl repeats. "What did I do?"

"Maybe the trees saw you fighting with Seth and Tyke, and—"

Carl interrupts me. "Saw?"

"Okay. Maybe *sensed*."

Aaron swipes his hand across his forehead, like he's making sure no X is there. "So, what do we do?"

"I need to get Fauna out. If the staff won't let me, we'll have to find a way."

Carl turns to Aaron. "If I keep not showing up at Math Wizards, they'll be suspicious."

Aaron is still fingering his forehead. "Don't worry, I can cover for you again."

"Thanks, man." Carl turns to me. "I'll help you."

Aaron clears his throat. "We should tell the police."

"Are you kidding?" Carl blurts. "They would interrogate Flora for weeks, and then they'd hand her over to people who'd conduct awful experiments on her." He picks up his phone. "You gotta see this." He taps the screen and I recognize the voice.

Aaron swallows. "Who's that?"

"It's my dad," I say. "He's a scientist, a botanist." It feels surreal to talk about my dad as if he's part of my life. "He just posted this video yesterday."

Aaron shakes his head, like it's all too crazy to take in. When the video ends, he looks at me. "What if it's happening now? This revolution?"

"Then this is just the start." The moment I say it, I realize I sound like my dad.

I suddenly notice how dark it's gotten and jump up. "Crap. My phone's dead. What time is it?"

"Almost 9:00," Aaron says, checking his watch.

I cringe. "I've got to get home." I hurry to the front door and the boys follow.

"I can walk with you," Carl offers.

"No. You have to be careful and stay out of sight. Can you stay here tonight?"

"Yeah," he says, and I mouth *thank you* to Aaron.

"But tomorrow . . ." I abruptly realize what I'm asking of him. "It might be too risky for you to help me."

"I have to try," he says. "I can't let the bravest girl I know face that care facility all alone. You're going to need an accomplice."

I smile. "Thanks, partner in crime."

Did he really just call me the bravest girl he knows?

Carl gives me a quick hug and his hands linger on my waist. "Just keep away from trees, flower-girl."

"I'll do my best," I say.

THE STREETS ARE strangely deserted—no cars on the road, no one walking their dog. The houses are stately in this part of town with their lush gardens. A giant maple tree up ahead stretches its limbs over a thick bamboo hedge, the dark branches swaying against a pale moon. There's barely a breeze, just the sticky night air against my skin.

But then I feel it: the tingling growing stronger in my lightning marks.

I brush up against a pointy bamboo leaf and hear *cut, cut, cut,* just like in the forest. I take off running, my sneakers slapping against the pavement. In the distance, a cat lets out a long wail.

As I approach the corner of the hedge, I'm panting but I think I hear faint voices.

I come to a hard stop. "Hello?" I say.

"Who's there?" It's a man's voice, loud and deep. I recognize it, but I can't quite place it.

"It's me. Flora Reed."

The next thing I know, the gleaming barrel of a gun is pointed at me. I freeze. The man holding the gun slowly appears from behind the hedge. His dark eyes fix on me, and a group of men, all carrying guns, materialize behind him.

"Mr. Dunne?" I begin taking a tentative step forward, but Mr. Dunne backs up. "It's me, Flora," I say.

"Stay where you are," he commands.

"It's Ava's girl," someone mumbles.

In my peripheral vision, I could swear I see the maple tree bending its branches toward us.

"You shouldn't be out here!" I warn, my lightning marks burning.

"Are you threatening us, girl?" I recognize the voice of Vice Principal Harrison, his cap pulled so low it nearly covers his face. And next to him is Mr. Owen, his hand on the gun in his holster.

"Please," I urge, "I'm warning you." My heart is racing, and my mouth is so dry, the words taste like dust.

"No, I'm warning *you*." Mr. Dunne takes a step closer. "If you see something, if you hear something—"

"You have to go home, all of you," I plead.

"Mike." Mr. Owen reaches for Mr. Dunne's shoulder. "Let her go."

Mr. Dunne lowers the rifle and I sprint past the men, past the whispering trees, to my street six blocks away, all the while wondering if seeing that maple tree move was truly only in my imagination.

32

FAUNA

"Not Flora," I beg them.

"Please, not my sister."

We still grow side by side. One with roots, one without.

I can feel her every breath, her frantic footsteps, her fear seeping into the darkness.

"Please, please, not my sister."

33

FLORA

I SLAM THE DOOR BEHIND ME, MY HEART BEATING like it wants out of my chest.

"There you are!" Mom says. "I was really worried." Her hands hug her favorite tea mug, the one I painted in fifth grade with happy face flowers. "Why didn't you answer my calls or messages?"

"Sorry." I throw myself into a chair. "My phone died." I rest my elbows against our pine kitchen table and it's like I'm seeing it for the first time. It's been here for as long as I can remember, but now the lines and knots in its rugged surface seem to speak to me—of times even farther back than my childhood, of days before I was born.

Mom sighs, with that wrinkle between her eyes. "I was worried sick. You need to let me know where you are, especially now." She gestures to the dark window. "The mayor's ordered a dusk-to-dawn curfew until the people responsible for these atrocities are arrested."

"Oh. Is that why there were men out with guns?"

Mom frowns. "So you saw them?"

I decide not to mention that I had one pointed at me only minutes ago and just utter, "Mm hm."

"Chuck Owen came by and told me they were rounding up people for a neighborhood watch committee."

"Oh yeah?"

The creases return to Mom's brow. "I hope they catch the culprits soon."

I swallow hard, not knowing what to say.

Mom opens the fridge and pulls out a slice of casserole on a plate. "You hungry?"

"Starved."

She pops it into the microwave and crosses her arms.

"Have you . . ." She draws out the word, like she's reluctant to continue. ". . . heard about the two other boys?"

I nod.

"Did you hear they were found not far from here?" Tears well in her eyes.

A part of me wants to cry too, wants to tell her everything. But she's dealing with enough as it is. When the microwave dings, I notice her hands shaking as she pulls the plate out and sets it in front of me.

"Yeah, I heard." I don't dare mention I saw them too.

"The whole town's talking about it . . . the 'tree-jackings,' they're calling them." She shakes her head. "Who could do such horrible things?" She fetches a fork for me, a glass of water. "Those boys were just kids. Same age as you."

Mom's macaroni casserole is my favorite, but the knot in my stomach is back, along with the haunting memory of Seth and Tyke in the birch tree—their empty eyes, the branches wrapped around their necks, the bloody X's in their foreheads. I push the plate away. "Sorry, Mom. I don't know how I can eat . . . with everything going on."

Mom sits opposite me and pats my hand. "You need nutrition. You can't just run on empty."

"I know."

"You need your strength, especially with all of this."

"I know."

She gives me her "motherly concern" look and I take a reluctant bite of the casserole.

She manages a sad smile, then brings her fingers together, interlacing them like a spiky roof. "And I hate to bring this up now, but I have to ask: Why didn't you tell me that Abigail quit?"

I swallow my bite and take a deep breath.

"And the geraniums?" She holds her hand over her head. "They were up to the ceiling! I've never seen anything like it. They were almost . . . otherworldly."

I realize I can't keep hiding things from Mom. She's seen some of these weird occurrences with her own eyes now. I wasn't planning to tell her anything tonight about what Carl and I discovered online, or what happened to him in the woods. But since I have every intention of bringing Fauna home from the care facility tomorrow, I don't think I can keep her in the dark any longer about my theory.

"Mom, I think . . . I think there might be a connection of some sort . . . between Fauna and plants."

Mom's eyes widen.

"Living things . . . nature. And I . . . I can sense it too."

Mom's face goes blank and she shakes her head slowly, like she sees a ghost behind me. "No, no, no . . . this can't be happening." She jumps up from the table and starts pacing and wringing her hands. When she stops and turns to me, she actually looks frightened. "Tell me you haven't inherited your father's lunacy."

I flinch. *My father's lunacy?*

"I couldn't bear it, Flora. You're the only one I have left."

I cross my arms hard over my chest. "I am *not* crazy."

My defiance seems to shake Mom out of her momentary frenzy. "I'm sorry," she says. "This has all just been too much."

I get up and put my arm around her shoulders. "I know . . . all of us are freaked out. But I need to tell you what I think's going on."

I guide her back into her chair and sit next to her. "Mom, Fauna talks to me. Not in words, but with . . . *things*."

"What do you mean? What kind of things?"

"Acorns. Flowers. I think she can communicate through nature."

I can see that Mom is having a hard time hearing this, but I go on anyway.

"I heard her calling for me. In the oak tree."

Tears fill Mom's eyes. "Don't do this, Flora. Your dad suffered from similar delusions. He would go on and on, obsessed with the 'awakening of nature.'" She pronounces the last words like they taste bad in her mouth.

"But you saw the geraniums," I say.

"I know, but . . ." She shakes her head, and tears spill down her cheeks. "I can't do this. Just stop, okay?"

"But Mom, the tree-jackings, you must see how—"

"Flora! I asked you to stop." She goes to the sink, her back to me. With sharp movements, she starts doing the dishes. Her silence brings me back to the fearful nights of my childhood.

Fauna's silhouette would appear in the crack of my door, her small voice asking to stay with me. She would crawl into my bed and I would hum till she fell asleep, trying to drown out the sounds of our parents fighting. Then I would tiptoe out of my room, careful not to wake her. On the landing, I would sink to the floor, my chin against my knees, listening to their arguments in the darkness.

What I remember most after he left is the silence.

Mom never talked about his leaving. She just zipped it up like it never happened.

Mom's voice pulls me back to the kitchen. Facing me with a dripping plate in her hand, she says, "There is always a natural explanation." She waves the plate at me with fiery eyes. "Always!"

"Yes!" I blurt. "Exactly."

She turns back to the sink. "Don't be smart with me."

I exhale audibly, then pick up the fork and take another bite of the casserole, suppressing a grin. *A natural explanation.* She said it herself.

When I'm finished, I take my empty plate to Mom and offer to help.

She doesn't answer, just pulls the plate from my hands.

I grab a towel from the drawer and start drying the dishes in the rack.

"Mom?"

No answer.

"I want to take Fauna out tomorrow."

She stops swirling the dishrag.

"Just for a little while," I plead.

She shakes her head. "Absolutely not. It's too risky. What if she has another seizure?"

"But I would be careful."

"Careful," she snorts. "If you'd been more careful, then maybe Fauna wouldn't have—"

I immediately feel like I've been punched in the stomach.

She turns to me. "Honey, I didn't mean . . ."

But it's too late. I know what she meant, that she blames me for Fauna's accident.

The glass I'm drying slips from my hand and falls to the floor, breaking into countless pieces. I don't even try to pick up the jagged shards. Instead, I run upstairs to my room and curl up on the floor with my back against the door, like I can keep it all out if I press hard enough, wondering if Dad ever felt the same way.

34

FAUNA

I feel their pain and their confusion and their fear and their despair.

There's nothing I can do.

I can only count them, as the struggle subsides. It comes to me through the roots: every last tremble, every last breath.

One.

Two.

Three.

Four.

35

FLORA

"FLORA."

Dad wakes me, his forefinger over his lips. "Don't say anything."

I get up slowly, careful not to awaken Mom and Fauna sleeping beside me on a blanket under the oak tree. My little sister is just a baby, and she's been fussing all night, keeping Mom up. Now they are in a deep sleep, Mom with her arms around Fauna, and Fauna with her ginger head on Mom's chest.

Dad takes my hand and leads me through dewy grass that tickles my ankles. He kneels down by the door to the old shed, his eyes narrowed into a smile. "I want to show you something."

He unlocks the door and together we enter the tilted building, lined with shelves of pots and jars, smelling like mold and dirt. Giant bags of soil stand in the corner, and a variety of garden tools rest against one wall. On a crippled desk propped up with a stool sit a dozen clay pots. Inside each one are green sprouts raising their arms like they're greeting us.

"Look, Dad." I smile and turn to him, but he isn't there. The inside of the shed suddenly gets darker. Shadows seem to reach for me. "Dad! Where'd you go?" I spin around and look for him, but he's gone.

I blink awake, my heart racing. I'm in my bed. The sun is peeking in and the birds are chirping outside my window.

I untwist myself from the covers and sit up. *Was it a dream?* But it was so real. I can still remember the smell of mold and dirt and my father's hand around mine. It feels more like a vivid memory than a dream.

Your father's lunacy. Mom's words linger in my mind like an old wound split open. I reach for my phone. Still dead. *Crap, I forgot to charge it.* I crawl out of bed and plug it in. More of Mom's words replay in my mind. *If you had been more careful, then maybe Fauna wouldn't have . . .*

I close my eyes to shut out the bright summer morning and feel the air leave my lungs. At the end of the exhale is a pause, a floating moment where time stands still, ever so briefly, where I can empty myself of harsh words and heavy memories. And then I breathe in and open my eyes.

Today I will bring Fauna home. Mom can't stop me.

But first, I have to find out what my dad wanted to show me.

WHEN I COME downstairs, there are no glass shards, just golden rays of sunshine across the floor and a note for me on the kitchen table.

I didn't have the heart to wake you. Will you please come to the Book Nook when you're ready? Love, Mom

My eyes linger on Mom's precise handwriting, thinking it's strange how a thin piece of paper can feel this heavy in my hand. I know she wouldn't like it, what I'm about to do. She would ask me to not go digging into the past. In fact, she's probably hidden the key.

I pour myself a glass of orange juice and open the key cabinet. The keys feel like old friends as I run my fingers along the jagged teeth: the spare set to the Book Nook and our house, Grandma and Grandpa's house in Pensacola, their cabin in Lake Harmony, the lock for my old bicycle that I outgrew years ago. But the one I'm looking for isn't here.

I down my juice and open the junk drawer. It's filled with the usual stuff: dry rubber bands, cracked pens, wrinkled receipts, crooked bobby pins, some of my old, childish drawings that make me cringe. I spot a curled-up takeout menu from the local pizza parlor in the back and pull it out.

Then I run my hand across the back of the drawer. In one corner, I feel smooth, ornate metal and slide it toward me.

I pull out a key that looks as old as our house and hold it up. *If this is the key to the shed, I can't believe it was this easy.*

As I make my way across our expansive backyard to the far end, I remember Dad saying his grandfather built the farm and named it Pine Ridge. When Dad was a boy, this property was all farmland. But his father, Grandpa Nick, had no interest in farming. He wanted to pursue mathematics, science, botany, just like Dad ended up doing. So he sold the land in parcels to finance his academic interests, and that's when the other houses on our street were built. I remember Dad telling me how much Grandpa Nick loved the oak tree; he even put in his will that it couldn't be cut down. After Grandpa died in a freak electrical accident, Grandma Ruth raised Dad on her own, and she cherished the oak tree all the more. After she died, when I was four and Fauna only one, our family moved back here to Dad's childhood home.

It's a charming old house, on a magical piece of land, but I think Mom has grown to hate it. Every day, she has to look at the tree that Fauna fell from.

I let the tall grass tickle my palms, and the familiar tingling travels up the back of my hands and arms, like muffled whispers from far away. I feel like a little girl again out here;

it's like my life started here by the meadow and the woods behind our house, not in the apartment in West Philadelphia we lived in before we moved here. It was in this outdoor arena that I started painting, spending long hours in the meadow mixing watercolors to find the right shades of sky blue and forest green—back when I dreamed of becoming an artist, of strolling through an art gallery filled with my paintings, of something beautiful I had created.

When I reach the other side of the yard, I look back at our house and am filled with a feeling of make-believe. From this distance, our home looks like a dollhouse, with tiny potted plants in the windows. I wish I could pick Fauna up and place her in her room and make everything alright again. I wish I could do the same with Dad.

The old shed is covered in vines and deep thickets that block the entrance. It's difficult to clear a path, and the tingling in my arms is growing stronger and stronger.

Finally, I find my way to the door and try the key.

It slides right in. One turn, two turns, *click*.

The hinges are rusty and I give the door a hard shove with my shoulder. It emits a wail and I tumble inside. The scents of mold and dirt immediately accost me, just like in the dream. All of the windows are overgrown with vines, casting a dim, greenish light. I can imagine Carl saying how whopping freaky it is in here, and I have to smile. That boy makes me smile even when he's not here.

The wilderness has found its way in—vines climb the

walls and wind themselves over shelves full of moldy pots, jars, and weird equipment. A massive table covered with dusty books and more pots stands in the middle, with what looks like a rusty car battery with black cables biting into it, their tails curling over the edge. I touch the withered remains of a potted plant and the stem is so dry that it collapses into dust.

I am startled by rustling and hold my breath. I exhale and smile when I see it's a blue jay. "Hey, there," I say. I scan the shed for a cracked window but don't see one.

The bird settles on a top shelf and fixes its eyes on me.

"Thanks for the acorns," I say, then add with a chuckle. "You haven't seen my dad in here, have you?"

The blue jay tilts its head.

I sigh. "I wish I knew what happened. Why he disappeared." My voice seems to dissolve into the green shadows as I step farther inside and survey the scene. It looks deserted, like someone was working here doing research or experiments, and then suddenly whisked away. A notebook is lying open, smeared in dirt and dust. I gently brush it off and it makes me cough. The paper is damp and soft, like a wet watercolor painting, and I handle it carefully so it won't rip. Under the spots of black mold, I can discern my father's handwriting: drawings, doodles, numbers. Pressed against the page is a single flat oak leaf, faded into a grayish sage. I gingerly lift the leaf and see that underneath it, Dad has drawn a tree with a wide trunk and majestic crown. *Our oak tree.* But in the drawing, part of the tree is cut away to the core of the trunk, with crooked lines leading to notes in the margins. The words are smudged, but I can make out *linguistic, cortex, tree-talk.* In the heart of the tree, he's drawn a dark line, like a spine or a rod of some sort.

Was Dad experimenting on the oak tree?

It definitely feels like there's something significant here —but also something important that I'm missing. The blue jay chirps in the corner, and my lightning marks flare up in a throbbing pulse.

I pull my phone from the pocket of my jeans and take a picture of the drawing, then another of the tabletop. I snap a few more of the crammed, dusty shelves and the vines so lush, they seem to be growing while I photograph them.

Was this what my father wanted to show me in the dream, like a memory? The place where he first explored The Natural Intelligence Revolution?

The YouTube video!

I bring up the page on my phone and scroll through the comments. But there's no answer from him, just one new comment below mine that says, "Is this guy for real?"

I notice the blue jay has gone quiet and look up toward the shelf where it sat only moments ago. I don't see him, but I would have heard him if he flew off somewhere. I step closer and squint. *It can't be.* The blue jay is caught in the vines, its head at an odd angle.

Images of boys entangled in trees flash before me,

branches hugging their bodies, the same way the vines appear to be squeezing the small chest of the bird before my eyes.

The blue jay was trying to warn me.

I back away, stumbling against the table, my arm flailing for the door. But the vines have already overtaken it from the inside. I shove my hand into the greenery and fumble for the handle. Stems wrap around my wrist, whispering, *cut, cut, cut.* I find the cold metal of the handle and pull on it, but the door won't move.

I spin around and search the shed for something, anything, sharp or pointed. I see a spade and grab it, then swipe at the vines until the blade clangs against the door and it swings open.

Panting, I rush out into the sunshine and turn around just in time to see the vines reach for the door and pull it closed with a long, ghoulish squeal.

36

FAUNA

The battle cry, coming through the roots.

"Cut, cut, cut."

"Not Flora," I shout in every shade of green, but creepers are a different kind, grass too, and they don't listen.

"Please, you already took the others, not my sister too."

37

FLORA

RUN, I TELL MYSELF.

Run!

The tall grass seems to reach for me like masses of thin fingers clinging to my arms, my waist, my ankles. I hear them now, a thousand voices screaming in my skin. *Cut, cut, cut.*

It's all around me: the forest, the meadow.

Your father's lunacy.

The gravel of our driveway is now under my feet, the branches of our oak above me. I stumble to the trunk and throw my arms around it, pressing my cheek against the rough bark. Here the pulse is calmer, a steady falling and rising. I can feel it in my skin like music, like breathing. And there it is, over and over.

Flora. Flora.

"Fauna," I whisper, "please help me understand." but my words don't seem attuned to the voice of the tree, like we're speaking different languages. Yet the current, the tingling, the pulse seems to be desperately trying to say something. *I need Fauna.*

I pull my hand along the lightning scar in the bark, like a goodbye. "I'll be back," I say.

I take off running again down Pine Ridge Road. Mrs. Walsh is outside her cottage, cutting her climbing roses. She hears me coming and waves with her hand pruners.

"Good morning!"

I am about to return her greeting when I see what appears to be blood on her face. I stop and motion to my forehead. "Do you realize you're . . ."

"What, dear?"

She turns to me and it is unmistakable. Across her forehead is a large X.

"You're . . . you're bleeding," I stammer.

"Oh, it's nothing." She holds out her scratched arms. "Happens all the time."

I rush up to her. "Mrs. Walsh." I grab her wrinkled hand. "You need to get inside and stay inside."

"But it's such a lovely morn—"

"Please," I interrupt her. "Will you just do it?"

"But why?"

She'd think I was crazy if I tried to explain. *Your father's lunacy.* "Please, just trust me."

I give her a gentle push from behind then break into a run again. There's barely anyone out, and when I turn onto Main Street, half of the shops are still closed.

I push open the door to the Book Nook, the merry jingle once again not matching the mood. Mom is bent over a large box on the floor, unpacking a batch of new books.

"There you are, honey."

We haven't talked since last night, and she comes straight to me, as if to offer her regret. When she wraps me in her arms, though, it feels like a leftover hug, stiff and stale, the words still hanging between us like an invisible wall.

If you'd been more careful, then maybe Fauna wouldn't have...

I pull away to catch my breath. "Mom, you have to stay here, inside the store."

Alarm crosses her brow. "Why? What's going on?"

"The grass in our backyard," I start. "... and the roses."

Mom tips her head with a deeper furrow.

"I'm trying to tell you," I implore. "There's something going on, with nature ... everywhere."

Mom grabs my shoulders. "Flora, you *have* to stop this."

The bell jingles and Mrs. Owen tumbles breathlessly into the shop. She falls into the corner armchair, her pungent perfume leaving a trail in her wake. "Did you hear?"

My heart sinks. *Carl.*

Mom rushes over to her. "What's wrong, Phyllis?"

"There've been more." Mrs. Owen's voice is hoarse. "Tree-jackings, I mean. Four of them." She brings her hand to her heart, panting between sentences. "Over by the high school, behind the football field. They were part of the neighborhood watch committee, out there trying to protect us. Thank goodness my Chuck is alright."

I realize I've been holding my breath. "But Carl? He's okay, right?"

"I hope so. I haven't seen him since yesterday morning. He's always coming and going. I never know what he's up to. He's not even answering his phone." She turns to Mom. "Chuck said the group that got tree-jacked were volunteers from the PTA. Poor souls, isn't it awful?"

I'm so relieved that Carl wasn't one of them, but Mrs. Owen's last word lingers. I *do* feel awful. And guilty too that I just drew a breath of relief when four people will never breathe again.

"Who could possibly do such awful, awful things?" Mrs. Owen cries.

Mom has been silent, but now she looks at me. "There *must* be a natural explanation." She's trying to sound reasonable, but she has the same panic in her eyes as last night when when she told me about my father's obsession with the awakening of nature.

"A serial killer." Mrs. Owen hisses the words, like pronouncing them might conjure the killer. "I'm on my way to the town hall to see what will be done about it."

Fleeting images of four limp bodies entangled in trees pass before my eyes, the scratched faces, the bleeding wounds. I swallow, feeling like I'm going to be sick.

"We're all sitting ducks," Mrs. Owen says. "This whole town."

Suddenly, a loud *thump* hits the window. Then another. Egg yolks crawl down the glass in yellow blobs. Mom runs to the door and flings it open.

"Damn it!" she says. "They're gone already."

Mrs. Owen stands and huffs. "We all have to be careful. These are strange and dangerous times." Then she slips out the open door and hastens down the sidewalk.

"Mom," I say with urgency, dragging her away from the door.

"Will you help me clean—"

"Mom. I really need to talk to you."

"Flora, I've told—"

CRASH. We both hit the floor and cling to each other. Glass is everywhere. A rush of adrenaline sends me out the broken door, the glass pane now a gaping mouth with jagged teeth.

"Who did this?" I scream. "Who did this?" I barely recognize the fierceness of my own voice. I catch a glimpse of someone disappearing around the corner, near Betty's Bakery.

"Hey, stop!" I call out, chasing after them. But by the time I reach the corner and scan the intersection and the backstreets, I only see a garbage collector emptying trash into his truck.

I hurry back to the Book Nook, where Mom is still

crouched on the floor. I sink down beside her. "I didn't get them."

Mom is holding something in her lap. She lifts it with trembling hands: it's a brick with a wrinkled note wrapped around it. There is only one word scribbled on it in black marker.

WITCHES

38

Fauna

Come find me.

   I am right around the corner.

   Not there, not there.

   But here.

   I am here.

   So close that you can feel me if you shut your eyes, count to ten, search for me with your hands outstretched in the dark.

   Come find me.

39

FLORA

"I HAVE TO CALL CHIEF BATISTA," MOM SAYS.

"And I have to go to Fauna," I say.

I notice Mom's batik blouse has a tiny tear in the seam, and I place my hand lightly over it, like I could heal the tear in her heart. "To make sure she's alright," I whisper.

I step carefully between the pieces of glass.

"Yes. You go talk to her," I hear Mom say.

I turn around and see a trace of a smile in her pained eyes. *Talk to her.* Just like that, she tore down the wall between us. I smile back at her, then crunch through the broken shards and out the door.

Before I head down the street, I glance into the shop window. It frames the image of my mom, distorted by smears of egg, pulling herself to her feet. My heart is filled with an aching warmth knowing she will sweep the floor and clean the window, like she took care of Fauna and me all on her own after Dad left—like she always takes care of everything with her silent resilience.

I pull out my phone to text Carl.

On my way to Fauna now
Can you make it?

I don't even have to look up. I can already feel the blossoming linden trees whisper in my lightning marks, and I break into a run across the tiny yellow flowers blanketing the sidewalk.

Half the shops are still closed, and the girl from the coffee shop across the street is pulling down the shades. It's after ten; normally they would have opened by now.

The news has obviously traveled fast.

I cross the intersection, and as I pass the white oak tree, an elderly couple climbs the stairs to the town hall, the bent man pressing a bloody napkin to his forehead.

When I reach the awning of White Oak Manor, I stop to catch my breath, then push the heavy door open. No one is at reception. *Perfect.* I hurry down the corridor, where I hear Rhonda's voice spilling from the room across the hall from Fauna's.

Silently, I slip through Fauna's door. She is still in her bed, her ginger hair spread over the pillow. *Didn't anyone help her get dressed?*

"Fauna, it's me," I whisper. I stroke her hair and am certain there's a glimpse of a smile. "I'm bringing you home with me today."

The geraniums, still absurdly big and boasting every shade of pink, look cramped with their necks bent under the ceiling, like something out of a fairytale.

"Flora, thank goodness!" Rhonda bursts through the door. "We're terribly understaffed today. People calling in sick, not showing up at all, it's been a crazy morning."

"Oh . . . so . . ." I stammer, "you wouldn't mind me bringing Fauna home for the day?" I try to sound casual, but Rhonda's face immediately spells concern.

"In her condition? With everything going on in town? You heard about the new tree-jackings, right?"

I need to find a reason good enough for Rhonda to accept, but she is already shaking her head.

"I really can't advise it." She motions to the hallway. "Especially today."

I bite my lip. *This won't be easy.*

Right on cue, my phone belts out the intense strings of Vivaldi's *Summer*—Fauna's favorite.

"Sorry," I say, pulling out my phone. "It's my mom."

As I step into the corridor, I hear Rhonda's resonant voice say, "Alright, honey, let's get you out of bed."

"Mom?" I press my phone to my ear.

"Flora, I don't know what to tell Chief Batista. He's on his way here."

"Just tell him everything."

"Every. Thing?" She splits the word in the middle, like she'd rather tell him half and no more.

"Yes. This is not going to just go away. In fact, I think—"
I swallow.

"You think what?"

Your father's lunacy.

But I'm *not* crazy.

If nature is awakening . . .

I finish the thought out loud. "This is just the beginning."

I hear her draw a deep breath.

"Mom, I have to go."

She exhales. "Okay, then. But *please*, be careful."

Rhonda squeezes past me. "I'm sorry, Flora. I have to deal with an issue. I've got Fauna sitting in her favorite spot in her wheelchair, but I didn't have time to get her dressed. Do you think you could do it?"

"Sure. Don't worry about it," I say, hoping I've just been given my perfect window to sneak Fauna out.

I wriggle her out of her pajama top and into her gray sweatshirt. The pants will take too much time, though, so I leave her pajama bottoms on and slide her feet into socks and sneakers. Her hair is messy, so I quickly comb through her soft curls with my fingers, parting them into three sections, then pull a hairband from my wrist to finish her thick braid.

"Time to go home, Fauna."

Her pale blue eyes stare straight ahead, but I can feel my lightning marks tingle, the connection between us getting stronger.

I check my phone. Still nothing from Carl. I worry that he's alright, since it's not like him to not show up. But I can't wait any longer. I'll have to do this alone.

I scan the hallway. I hear voices in the distance but no one is visible. As I push Fauna out of her room, I have the eerie sense that the geraniums tilt their pink heads in our direction.

I am hurrying down the hall when Rhonda's voice booms from reception. "We're already understaffed, I cannot—"

Crap. Before Rhonda sees us, I steer Fauna into a small sitting room to my right, with French doors leading to the garden. Ms. Mayfair is sitting on a sofa, staring ahead with her blind gaze. I try the doors but they're locked.

"Wait here, Fauna," I whisper. When I spin around, Ms. Mayfair is standing so close to me, I'm staring into her unseeing eyes.

"Oh, you scared me, Ms. Mayfair."

"I may be blind, but I can hear." Her voice is raspy, like it's the first time she's spoken in a long time. She reaches for me and softly traces the lightning marks on my arm. "I hear them calling your name," she says. "Flora."

Her touch sends a tremor all the way to my neck. "Who?" I ask her.

She leans in and I feel her warm breath in my ear. "All of them," she says. "The night creatures, the frogs, the bats, even the moonlight."

"You hear them . . . talk to you?"

Ms. Mayfair raises her hands and pulls her gray hair apart, revealing a thin scar the shape of a crescent moon. "You're not alone," she says. "There are more of us who can hear nature in all of her wonderful languages—the night, the trees, the soil, the water. You need to find them. You need the young ones, the ones who can fight."

I stare at her scar. It's flat and pale. She must have gotten it a long time ago. I'm aware that time is ticking but I don't have a key to the door anyway. If Rhonda finds us in here, I'll just say I was taking Fauna for a stroll.

"What happened to you?" I ask.

"I fell into a dry well on my father's farm when I was eight. That's how I lost my eyesight. I hit my head and was trapped down there for days before they managed to get me out." Her pupils dart back and forth, as if she can see her childhood home. "At first I resisted the darkness. I screamed and screamed until I could hear it scream back at me. And then I learned to listen. I never knew fireflies had that much to say." She brings her thin hands, light as tiny birds, to my shoulders. "I've been listening for you and your sister. Remember: the seed grows where it's planted. It all comes back to the seed." She tears up. "Flora, you're the one."

My eyes grow large. "The one?"

"To tell them that the trees are not our enemies."

Ms. Mayfair pulls me into an embrace. "Bless you, child." When she releases me, she pulls a key out of her dress pocket with a cunning smile.

My silence must alert her to my surprise. She chuckles. "No one expects the blind to pick pockets."

I take the key. "Oh my gosh . . . thank you."

I unlock the door, and when I swing it open, the garden is all chirping and sunlight. For a brief moment, I wonder if life will ever be the same as before, when I could look at nature and not scan every shrubbery, tree, and patch of grass, searching for possible threats.

You're the one echoes in my mind.

"Okay, Fauna," I whisper, "here we go."

The wheelchair is heavy, but I manage to push it over the threshold and onto the uneven stones of the patio, then faster across the trimmed lawn. Daisies are peeking up as we pass, like arrows pointing directly to us. But thankfully, we seem to go undetected as we enter the narrow alley that runs parallel to Main Street.

As I zoom past a dumpster, the wheelchair catches on a piece of plastic sticking out, making it skid. I dash around to pull it out of the way, and when I bend down I hear, "Hey, flower-girl, I've been looking for you."

I look up to find Carl smiling down at me, all dimples and white teeth under the red Phillies cap. As usual, he's got his backpack over his shoulders, the gray of his t-shirt against his dark skin highlighting the taut muscles of his arms. I can't help throwing my arms around him. "I thought you weren't coming."

I can tell he's been running. "Sorry I'm late. The police

are all over town. I had to literally run around in circles. I didn't know where I'd find you."

I smile. "But somehow you did."

He gives me a wink. "I'd never stand you up, flower-girl." He grabs the handles of Fauna's wheelchair. "Hey, Fauna, nice day for a ride."

I love how he talks to my sister like he knows her, even though they never met before the accident. He steers Fauna down the alley, past the back door of the Book Nook, then stops behind Betty's Bakery at the sound of sirens.

"Did you hear about the new tree-jackings?" I ask.

"Yeah. It was on the local news this morning."

The wailing fades and we cross the road, hurrying along the backstreets until we're out of downtown Derwyn.

Carl and I switch places and he pulls his phone from his pocket. "I searched for similar events, people found dead in trees and such. There was this interesting blog post—" He stops by the hawthorn hedge. "*What?!*" His fingers move like spider legs over his phone. He looks at me and shakes his head. "They freakin removed them. Look."

He shows me the *Page not found* message.

"*They?*" I say. "Who?"

He slips his phone into his pocket. "Someone who doesn't want people to know what's happening here."

40

FAUNA

You are so close.

I can already sense your heart against mine, your ear pressed to my cheek.

The words streaming between us like they used to.

Only this time they are words of warnings and promises, fire and ashes, reunions and goodbyes.

41

FLORA

CARL PUSHES FAUNA AROUND THE HAWTHORN hedge and I abruptly grab the back of the chair.

"Wait," I say.

I have no idea how Fauna will respond to being home for the first time since the accident, if she'll respond at all. The scarred oak tree; our old farmhouse with its gray, weathered siding; the overgrown yard crowded with wildflowers and bushes, all in plain view for her.

Like always, Fauna sits practically motionless. But she's not staring straight ahead. She has tilted her face up toward the sky, like she's listening to music only she can hear.

She must know she's home.

"Okay," I tell Carl. "Let's do this."

We push her onto the grass, over the thick roots of the oak tree, getting as close to it as we can manage.

"What can I do?" Carl asks.

"You can lift her out and prop her against the tree."

My heart aches as Carl picks up Fauna. She is so thin that her limbs are like twigs in her clothes. But her thick ginger braid and pale blue eyes are exactly the same. Apart from her frailty, and without the wheelchair, she looks just the way she did before the accident.

I wipe a tear from my cheek as Carl says, "Like this?" He has set Fauna down between two large roots, her back against the trunk.

"Yes, that's perfect." I sink down next to my sister and wrap an arm around her shoulder. As soon as I do, burning pulses charge through me, through Fauna, through the oak tree, as if we are one being. It is so strong I can barely breathe.

"You alright?" Carl says.

His voice seems to come from far away and I can't answer him. I can only close and open my eyes. With each blink, the world looks different, the colors sharper. I see details I never noticed before: the veins and arteries of every leaf, the kneecaps of a ladybug, the stag beetle drinking sweet sap from bark. I not only see them, I *feel* them—the struggle, the hunger, the fear, but also the joy of being alive. Most of all I feel the steady cadence of the oak coursing through the leaves, the trunk, the roots, then through the ground to the forest across the meadow. It's unbelievable: I actually feel *every tree* in the forest—along with every one that came before it and will ever come after it.

Suddenly the years blur together—a decade, a century, a millennium. It's all a flicker of a leaf.

And there's something else, something that evokes deep emotion within me. I feel how much the tree loves me. It is as if the tree knows me, has always known me, and will always know me. I gasp for air and feel like I'm tumbling out in space, like it's all too much.

I turn to Fauna.

She is smiling at me.

Trembling with awe, I take her hand.

She inhales deeply. Then, with a long exhale, she says, "Flor-a."

As she draws out my name, I feel the oak calling me too, like a current that runs through my lightning marks, causing a door to open in my mind, a door I didn't even know existed.

"Flora," Fauna repeats slowly, and the oak echoes her. "We don't have much time."

I shoot a look at Carl, who is as stunned as I am.

"Is it really you?" I whisper.

A smile spreads across her face. "I never left. I've been here the whole time." Her eyes look right into mine, her soft voice a melody I never thought I'd hear again.

"I'm so sorry I didn't find you sooner," I say.

Her voice is a gentle breeze, caressing my ear. "How could you know?"

I stroke her hand softly. "I've missed you so much."

I immediately realize we no longer need words to communicate; I can feel in my skin that she's missed me too. I sense her every lonely afternoon in White Oak Manor, every longing for her home and her family, every time she wished to speak to me but couldn't.

"I am so, so, sorry, Fauna," I say, tilting my head against hers.

She lingers for a moment, then twists slightly. I instinctively know it's not because she's pulling away from me, but because she has things to say, important things. I can feel them like birds flapping their wings, about to land.

"Don't be sorry," she says tenderly. "This is a gift." The clarity of her eyes is breathtaking. "You're wondering why trees are cropping humans."

She knows my question even before I ask it, just like the tree does, communicating Fauna's same words in my mind like an echo, or like a reverent confirmation.

I'm aware of Carl witnessing all of this as Fauna's bright eyes envelop me.

"They're trying to protect you."

We're trying to protect you.

"Protect us?" I ask.

Fauna nods.

Warn you.

"Of what?"

She inhales deeply. "Of Day X."

My eyes grow wide. "What's that?"

But Fauna and the oak are already feeding me the answers in anticipation of my questions. I can feel myself learning the rhythm, the language, of how the oak's knowledge pours like crystal clear water from the heart of the tree, through the bark and into my arms, my hands, my mind.

They tell me that Day X is the day it's too late—when nothing can be done to save the Earth. It is the season of withering and rot, of leaves losing their color and falling to the ground for the last time, when spring never appears again.

I both feel it and see it: the suffocating smoke, the flames licking the tree trunks, the leaves curling up and crackling. I see sap boiling in the trees' veins as insects seek shelter by crawling deeper into the bark, only to be roasted in their nests. I feel the teeth of the machines grinding through limbs, the roots crying in pain, the green canopies erased, the wind howling between the mutilated tree stumps.

Then I'm shown seeds retreating into poisoned ground, rust tainting the water, dead animals floating in the streams. I see mountains of trash, desert dunes filled with plastic and metal, corrosive liquids bleeding into the soil. I see children rummaging through trash, swimming in polluted creeks, rooting through gravel for food, breathing black smoke that makes their hollow chests cramp with every breath.

And then . . .

I see no children. Only a wasteland from horizon to horizon, gray stretches of land under an eternally gray sky.

And then nothing.

Nothing but an unending winter on an uninhabitable planet, an infertile orb floating in space, like a seed without soil or water.

I feel as if I'm floating into blackness, and I can't breathe for the pain in my chest, my lungs, my heart.

All that beauty, all that struggle, all that love, all that knowledge, all that experience, all those lives . . . it is all gone.

Slowly, I emerge from the vision and feel Fauna's hand on my chest, feeding air back into my lungs. Carl is crouched next to me, his hand wrapped around mine.

Fauna says, "So, you see . . . I was put here for a reason. And you're here for a reason too."

I nod and feel Carl squeeze my hand.

"You and I," Fauna continues, "we're the bridge between two civilizations that have been living side by side for millennia, but never really learned to speak to each other." She takes her hand from chest. "My destiny is fulfilled. Now it's up to you."

My eyes brim with tears and I can't stop them from streaming down my cheeks. "Don't talk like that. I'm going to save you. I'll find a way to make you whole again."

Fauna gives me a faint smile. "I love you, Flora." Her voice trembles. "And tell Mom I love her too."

I feel her start to pull away from me. "You'll tell her yourself," I say, trying to push the words into the energetic connection we share. "You'll tell her."

Fauna looks at me tenderly. "We need to go back," she says. "Your moment is approaching."

"But if we leave, you won't . . ." My voice breaks.

She picks up an acorn from the ground and puts it in my

hand, closing my fingers around it. "Remember the acorns. They fall off the tree and into the soil where they sprout into new beings, new trees. It will be like that, like a rebirth. We will meet again." Fauna smiles at me, then turns and places both hands on the tree trunk. With a groan, she firmly pushes herself away and falls into the grass.

The moment she's no longer touching the tree, she's gone. She returns to being the Fauna whose expressionless eyes gaze into the distance, the same vegetative girl as after the accident. My Fauna, in the blink of an eye, is like a butterfly fallen to the ground.

Just then, a tremor runs through the crown of the oak. The leaves rustle, and I can feel Fauna in my lightning marks.

She's still here.

"I'll get you back, Fauna," I tell her. I lift my face to the pattern of sunlight and shadow, leaves and branches, things seen and unseen, where she resides. "I'll get you back."

The tree pours an infinite sadness through my skin, traveling up my arms and filling my heart. I flinch and pull away, and Carl takes me in his arms.

"You'll get her back," he assures me.

The leaves of the oak twist and quiver.

Even though I resist it, I know they are whispering the answer to the question I refuse to ask.

42

FAUNA

To feel your hand in mine.
  To speak to you.
  My beloved sister.
  One more time.
  Thank you.
  Thank you.
  Thank you.

43

FLORA

I WATCH CARL LIFT FAUNA FROM THE GROUND. AS soon as he does, dandelions and daisies sprout up where she lay. It is remarkable to see, yet on this strange day, it is the least strange thing that has happened.

I reach out and caress the flowers, feeling their love for my sister, until slowly they close their petals and bend their heads under the palm of my hand in a silent goodbye.

I slide the acorn Fauna gave me into the pocket of my jeans as Carl places Fauna in her wheelchair. I adjust her legs and feet, then make sure her hands lie comfortably in her lap.

Without saying a word, Carl and I each take a handle and start back to White Oak Manor.

I can't help but wonder what Carl must be thinking after what he just witnessed. Even though he was right there, holding my hand and not running away, what if he's finally realized what a freak I am? Maybe deep down, he wants nothing to do with all of this, with me, but just doesn't have the heart to say it.

I'm lost in my thoughts when Carl says, "Day X."

I turn to find him looking at me with that special fondness in his eyes.

"It's a lot to take in," he says.

My chin quivers. "So you heard her?"

We are just crossing the small bridge over the creek, and Carl stops and locks the wheelchair. He gently brushes hair from my face as the water murmurs beneath us. "I heard everything. I didn't want to intrude . . . but when you seemed to go . . . *somewhere else* . . . I had to go to you."

He pulls me close and I let his soft cotton t-shirt collect my tears. "We'll get her back again," he reassures me, the softness in his voice coming straight from his heart as he holds me.

I cling to his promise as much as to him, relieved by his understanding. When I finally pull away, Carl swipes a tear from my cheek with his thumb.

"There must be a way," he says.

I suddenly remember the photos I took earlier. "I think these might help us." I pull out my phone and show the pictures to Carl.

"Where did you find this stuff?"

"In my dad's old shed." I point to the gloomy photo of the table with its damp books and moldy pots. "It was full of his research. Tools and books and stuff. He was obviously working on something when he left. If we can find him, maybe he can help us."

"Yeah," he says, "maybe from that video." He studies the photos. "When were you in the shed?"

"This morning." The memory of the vines and the blue jay wring my heart. "It was actually pretty scary. I felt like the plants in there were out to get me." I force a laugh, but Carl doesn't smile. Instead he shakes his head.

"You're amazing, Flora." He hands me back my phone and our fingers brush against each other.

I smile, sensing Carl's entire being through that swift touch of our hands.

He takes off his cap. The bruising has started to subside, but the X in his forehead is still clearly visible. He pulls me close again. "Whatever happens, remember I'm on your side."

I can feel our every heartbeat, and I realize it didn't use to be like this—that I didn't use to feel *this much*. It's as if my senses have been heightened after communicating with Fauna through the oak tree.

Carl pulls back slightly. He looks into my eyes, and I sense he's going to kiss me. Then he leans in and presses his mouth onto mine. His lips are soft and gentle. I feel his fingers tracing my chin and then the line of my jaw. "You're wonderful," he whispers.

My heart is pounding. I've dreamed of Carl kissing me, but I couldn't have imagined it would feel this magical. I want to revel in it: the way he holds me, the scent of his skin, his touch, his words. Everything inside me knows he's being sincere. But there is also a nagging undercurrent, something

I feel like he's hiding from me. Somehow, though, I don't want to know. Feeling safe in his arms, I just want to stand here, on this bridge, in this moment, with my cheek against his chest and his arms around me for a long, long time.

After a few moments, Carl says, "You okay?"

I pull away and look up at him with a smile. "Yeah." I don't want him to think I am anything but happy in this moment. So I cast my niggling concern for the time being into the water beneath us and let it float away.

"Hey, isn't that where . . ." I say, pointing toward the trail behind the row of backyards, leading up the hill.

He nods and puts his cap back on. "Behind the gym."

I shudder. "But they must have taken the victims down by now."

"I'm sure they have."

We resume walking, both of us pushing Fauna. Above us, the tree branches weave a billowing green ceiling, leaking sunlight into golden puddles below our feet. My skin picks up a faint tingling, and from the corner of my eye I see the branches bending closer, closer, like they're watching us, following our every step.

"Come on," I say, speeding up.

When we reach the football field, we encounter the all too familiar scene of black-and-yellow police tape. A group of policemen and firefighters are huddled by the grove of trees behind the gym. The victims are no longer in the trees. Carl puts his arm around me.

"Come on, Flora, you don't need to see this."

I stare at my scuffed white sneakers as we walk, the images of burning forests, hungry children, a dead planet, replaying in my mind.

We are trying to protect you. Warn you.

And then, I sense more unspoken words. This time, though, they seem to be coming from Carl. *I wish I could tell her everything.*

No. I must be imagining it. Like Mom would say, there has to be an explanation.

We continue walking in silence toward White Oak Manor. As we near it, we are both alarmed to see the town square full of people, with more streaming up the sidewalks and in the street.

I turn to Carl in a panic. "What are we going to do?"

He pulls his cap down and lowers his chin to his chest. "I guess we'll have to try to blend in."

We crisscross between people, against the current that is moving toward the town hall, trying to get across the street. Momentarily stuck in the throng, a little boy puts his finger on the pattern of pale zigzags on my arm. "Look, Mommy!" I can sense his innocence, his curiosity, and I force a smile, but the woman next to him gives me a stern look and pulls him away.

"Stay away from her," she hisses. "She's *that girl.*"

44

FAUNA

Root to root, the word has spread.

"... She's the one ..."

"... The girl with a mark in her skin in the shape of a tree."

45

FLORA

I CAN FEEL MY SKIN TINGLING MORE AND MORE with every step toward the majestic white oak.

I stay close to Carl, hoping my scarred skin won't draw any more attention. I curse myself for not putting on a long-sleeved shirt this morning, anything to help me blend in more easily.

"Look," I whisper with a nod toward the security guard. He's stacking pallets in front of the oak tree's wide trunk, building a podium of sorts.

Carl stops and pulls Fauna's wheelchair closer to him. "Seems like there's going to be a speech."

A thin man in his forties steps onto the pallets, and I recognize his face from the endless election ads: our mayor, Wayne Fitzpatrick.

As two guys fumble around with audio equipment, the tingling in my skin grows stronger. I feel the need to warn the mayor about the white oak, warn everyone, but I highly doubt they'd listen. *Your father's lunacy.*

Aaron suddenly appears next to me. "Hey," he says, gently poking me with his elbow.

"Hey," Carl says. "You're not at Math Wizards?"

"Got cancelled. Hardly anyone showed up today."

"I'm glad you're here," I say. He flashes me a quick smile as Mayor Fitzpatrick's voice booms through the mic.

"Hello, everyone. First, I want to apologize for not being able to accommodate you all in the town hall, which is why we're having this impromptu meeting outside."

A murmur ripples through the crowd, swiftly followed by outcries.

"What are you doing about the killings?"

"No one is safe!"

"Have you caught the killer?"

Mayor Fitzpatrick shifts his weight and puffs up his chest. "I'll answer your questions to the best of my ability, one at a time." He puts his hands out to shush the crowd. "The police are working tirelessly to solve the heinous crimes that have afflicted our community over the past few days." He motions to his side, where Chief Batista and Officer Herrera are standing with two other policemen I don't recognize. I still don't know what Mom told the chief, if she told him anything about nature's awakening, and if so, how much.

My lightning marks are burning now. Once again, I feel like I should alert everyone, but I remain quiet.

Mayor Fitzpatrick continues. "To ensure the safety of

everyone, I must stress the importance of adhering to the dusk-to-dawn curfew. Last night's victims were all people from a neighborhood watch committee out on the streets at night." He pauses to scan the crowd. "I repeat, everyone must obey the curfew."

A man speaks up. "They were trying to protect us!" It's Vice Principal Harrison.

Mayor Fitzpatrick opens his mouth, but a woman's shrill voice rings out. "That's more than any of you have done!"

The crowd starts to shout again.

"They were heroes!"

"Seven people have died in three days!"

"I don't let my kids out of the house anymore!"

Mayor Fitzpatrick lowers his hands, like he's closing the lid on the conversation. "We are just concerned about your safety. This killer is ruthless and doesn't seem to need a motive, just the opportunity. We have one person of interest we'd like to speak to, but we haven't been able to locate him."

Carl. I fumble for his hand and he takes it, squeezing me hard. A low whisper travels through my lightning marks: *Protect her.* I hold my breath, certain I didn't imagine it.

"Hell, stop this dainty talk, we all know who you mean." It's Mr. Dunne, stepping onto the podium with his rifle.

Chief Batista frowns.

"Does anyone know where Carl Nielsen is?" Mr. Dunne booms. "Chuck? Phyllis?" He points at the Owens.

They shake their heads and Aaron's eyes catch mine.

We need to get out of here.

But it's too late. From the corner of my eye, I see someone step away from us, and then more people pull away, as if we're dangerous. "Isn't that him and that girl?" someone says. The crowd recedes like a tide, turning the four of us—Fauna, Aaron, Carl, and me—into a solitary island in the middle of them. I grab the handle of Fauna's wheelchair. *Whatever happens,* I think, *I have to keep her safe.*

Mr. Dunne heads toward us through the crowd.

"Run," I whisper to Carl, but he only squeezes my hand tighter and leans in close.

"I'm not leaving you, flower-girl."

Mr. Dunne is standing in front of us now. His chin is covered in dark stubble, his hair falls in greasy strands, and his wrinkled blue shirt is open over a stained white t-shirt.

"You're one hard bastard to track down," he scowls.

Carl stands firmly next to me.

"You killed my son!" Mr. Dunne spouts, circling us like a vulture. "You and—" He points to me. "*Her.*"

I can barely feel my fingers, Carl is squeezing my hand so tight. I keep hearing the words *protect her, protect her* in my mind, coming straight from Carl. Neither of us move.

"You think pulling around a pathetic imbecile in a wheelchair is going to help you. But guess what?" Mr. Dunne leans in. "I don't care!" In one swift movement, he raises his rifle and points it at us. "Admit it!"

Carl immediately releases my hand and steps to the side,

prompting Mr. Dunne to follow him with the rifle as the sole target, in order to protect me and Fauna.

Just then, Chief Batista comes trampling through the crowd like a provoked bull. "Lower your weapon," he says sternly, aiming his service gun at Mr. Dunne.

Mr. Dunne motions at Carl with his rifle. "Admit that you killed him!"

Carl slowly raises his hands. "But I didn't."

"Put down your rifle, Dunne!" Chief Batista insists.

But Mr. Dunne is in a frenzy. "I saw what you did to Jack! I saw the video." He is shaking, but he keeps the rifle aimed at Carl.

"I *didn't* kill him." Carl has started to tremble.

Chief Batista moves closer. "Put. Down. Your. Weapon."

Mr. Dunne remains locked on Carl.

"Please, Mike." It's a woman, sobbing. "Please don't."

Mr. Dunne hesitates at the voice of his wife.

"Don't do this, Mike," she pleads. "I lost my boy—" Her voice breaks. "I couldn't bear losing you too."

Mr. Dunne's chin trembles. "You shouldn't be here, Maggie."

In that moment, Chief Batista grabs the rifle and points it toward the sky. A shot echoes. Mr. Dunne clings to the rifle, but the chief elbows him in the chest and pulls the gun from his hands.

"Herrera!"

The female officer steps in and pulls Mr. Dunne's arms

behind his back, then clicks a pair of handcuffs around his wrists.

"Okay, people," Chief Batista says loudly. "Let's all calm down here."

Officer Herrera and the other two cops haul off Mr. Dunne as the crowd becomes a mass of distressed and dumb-founded mutterings.

The chief turns to Carl.

"Carl Nielsen, I'm going to need to bring you in for questioning."

46

FAUNA

"She is here," Mother Tree says, the great white oak in the town square, centuries old.

"All arrows pointing to this moment in time.

"Drawing closer, but the people are drawing closer too, muddling the image.

"They are running through time looking backward, carrying their losses, collecting them, ever weighing them down.

"Running, running, straight into the void."

47

FLORA

I WATCH HELPLESSLY AS CHIEF BATISTA GRABS Carl by the arm and escorts him away.

I turn to Aaron. "Can you keep an eye on Fauna for me?"

He nods. "Of course."

Fauna is gazing at the white oak, like she's intently studying its massive canopy. I caress the tiny freckles on her cheek. "I'll be right back," I say.

I have to stand up for Carl with Chief Batista, but the crowd is blocking which direction they went. Voices rise from the mumbling as I push through.

"What's happening?"

"Did they get the suspect, that boy Carl?"

"Where's Mike? What did they do to him?"

I am shocked when the next voice I hear is Chief Batista's. He has dragged Carl up to the platform and is speaking into the microphone. I don't understand why the chief would do this. *Is he making a spectacle of Carl?* But then he says, "Everyone calm down. Carl Nielsen is not a suspect at this point. We just want to hear what he's experienced over the past few days."

A man shouts, "That's the killer!"

Chief Batista extends his hand, like he's calming an unruly dog. "I repeat, he is not a suspect."

Officer Herrera climbs onto the podium and leans toward Chief Batista. She mumbles something in his ear.

"Right." Chief Batista straightens up, relaxing his shoulders. "I just got word that reinforcements from Chester County are on the way. We're committing all our resources toward solving these crimes."

A large man to my left shouts, "How come Mike's the one in cuffs, while the killer is standing there like a prize hog?"

"He's *not* the killer," I say, but he doesn't seem to hear me. He cups his hands around his bearded mouth and adds, "Why don't you give him a nice ribbon and a bow around his neck?"

A bunch of people laugh and someone else chimes in, "Or a rope."

I see Carl tense up. Chief Batista tightens his grip on Carl's arm as more hateful murmurs rise from the crowd.

"That bastard . . ."

"Someone should . . ."

"He's not from here . . ."

"Blow his brains out . . ."

I can feel my lightning marks pulsating. *I have to speak*

up. "He's not the killer!" I shout. Pushing through the crowd, I reach the platform and step up. Everyone's faces seem to bleed together like runny watercolors. "He is *not* a killer!" I repeat. The strength of my voice surprises me.

The mob falls silent. They are all looking at me.

I have to warn them.

"I know Carl isn't the killer," I say. "I know how they all died."

A collective gasp fills the air. My heart pounds and my mouth goes dry. I take a deep breath.

"I know how this will sound, but *please*, listen to me."

Behind me Carl whispers, "Flora, you don't need to do this."

But I *do* have to. I can feel it in my lightning marks, my every heartbeat, my bones, that this is my responsibility.

"It was the trees," I say.

The blur of faces moves as people turn to each other. I am painfully aware that nearly everyone is gathered under the white oak, within reach of its meandering branches.

"They're cropping humans, like we do them. It's a warning. They don't want to do it, but it's the language of violence we have taught them, and now they're speaking to us." I hold out my arms to show my skin covered in pulsating red zigzags. "I can hear them, the trees. They've shown me what will happen if we humans don't change our ways, if we don't become part of nature like everything else living on Earth. We've been exploiting it, but it can't go on forever. The day is coming when the effects, the damage we've done, will be irreversible. The trees have shown me everything."

Images of the wasteland flash before my eyes and my throat tightens.

"You have to listen to me. We will all die, *all* of us, every living thing on the entire planet—humans, animals, plants. That's what the trees are trying to tell us."

A group of high schoolers in the front are snickering as they film me with their phones.

And then one face in the crowd materializes. It's Mom. She's sobbing and I don't know if she's on my side or not. *Your father's lunacy.*

A heavy hand lands on my shoulder. "Miss Reed." It's Chief Batista, his voice soft. "Your mother told me about your . . . your delusions."

My heart sinks. "But I—"

Chief Batista gently pulls me back. He has left Carl to Officer Herrera and has apparently made restraining me his mission.

"No, it's the truth!" I try to resist his grip, but his hands are locked around my wrists.

Mom pushes her way forward. "Flora," she snaps, and I instantly know whose side she has taken. "You must realize—"

"No! It's *you* who don't realize!" I squirm against Chief Batista, but he's too strong. "You're all in danger! And soon it'll be too late! We must listen to the trees or we'll all die!"

The crowd erupts into laughs and snide comments, like a one-minded organism, a multi-headed monster talking to itself. Amidst it all, one statement reaches me, as if it's meant to be the most blatant assault of all: "Wasn't her father that crazy scientist?"

"My father is a genius!" I shout, my blood searing. "He saw this coming before anyone else!"

But no one is listening. They are in their own deluded world, intent on placing blame on Carl and me. I hear someone say, "Maybe they're in it together, two deranged psychopaths."

I struggle against Chief Batista's grip. *If only I could show them.*

Suddenly it comes to me. "Take off his baseball cap!"

Chief Batista sighs. "Miss Reed."

I stop fighting and look him in the eye. "Please, Chief?"

He sighs again, then nods to Officer Herrera. She pulls off Carl's Phillies cap in one swift movement. Everyone in view of him can't help but see the jagged, dry X in his forehead.

"He was also marked!" I shout. "If he's the one doing this, if he's the killer like you say, why would he mark himself?"

Chief Batista nods to the officers next to the police car. "Bring her in too."

"No! You have to listen to me!"

But the officers are already pulling me from the platform.

"We'll be alright, flower-girl," I hear Carl say.

But we won't be alright. I remember the wasteland that Fauna and the oak tree showed me, stretching on indefinitely, like the future we face if I don't convince them. I'm begging them to let me go when a sound unlike anything I've ever heard brings the officers to an abrupt halt. Everyone's eyes tilt upward.

Like a giant who has slept for a thousand years, the white oak is unfolding its limbs.

With an eerie creaking, one enormous, twisted bough swiftly lowers itself toward the stage. Carl starts to run but it's too late. The tree extends its crooked branches and closes them around Carl, then retracts like a piece of machinery, pulling him up and into its crown.

48

FAUNA

The arrows.

    Pointing to this place in time.

    Ever as firmly to the girl who can talk to trees.

    But then there's the boy.

    The arrows are trembling.

    And then they stop.

49

FLORA

"Noooooo!" I fight my way past the policemen, past Chief Batista, onto the platform. Carl is right above me, far out of reach. He is yelling and pulling at the branches that are suffocating him. "Help him!" I implore, but everyone is paralyzed by shock, staring up in disbelief.

Carl starts making choking sounds and I realize the tree must have him by the neck, that it's squeezing the life out of him. His punches are getting slower, his kicking waning.

I rush off the platform and throw myself at the wide trunk of the oak, wrapping my arms around it. "Let him go," I scream, "let him go." I can feel the words in my skin, the pulsating language that Fauna taught me, traveling through my lightning marks and into the tree.

Let him go, let him go. Please, please, let him go.

But no words come from the tree, only the cracking and creaking of its massive branches. I hug the trunk harder. *You have to understand me. You have to.*

Just then, the tree sends a message through my arms. I can sense the current carrying fire, sorrow, regret.

He is marked for cropping, it says, as if it is a decision that's been made and can't be revoked. The tree floods my mind with memories of seedlings and young trees, trampled and cut down to make room for roads and houses. Main Street, the town hall, the manor that carries the white oak's name. I can feel the tree's mourning, the longing and the pain running through its core. *They were marked,* the tree cries. *He is marked too. There is nothing I can do.*

I press my cheek against the furrowed bark of the trunk. *I am so sorry about your children.* Tears stream down my face. *Please, please, put him down. If you do, you'll always have an ally in me.*

The tree goes silent. The creaking ceases and I can feel its hesitation, a weakening in the pulse. A few moments later, I sense a quickening as the words course through my arms.

For you and Fauna.

The white oak lowers its branches, growling like a hound.

Remember me, it says, just before I let go of the trunk.

I rush to Carl as his limp body is placed on the ground. Groaning, the wooden claws loosen their grip and untwine from his chest and neck, then retreat upward.

I fall on my knees beside him. He has turned ashen and his lips are blue. His eyes are closed and his chest isn't moving. I pull him into my lap and beg: "Live, live, live. Breathe, breathe, breathe."

Finally, Carl coughs and turns on his side. His chest heaves with his first breaths and his eyes flutter open. I let out an exhale as I bend over him. "I thought you were gone," I blubber.

He moans and looks up at me with his dark, tender eyes. "I told you I wouldn't leave you." His voice is so hoarse he can barely speak, but still he adds with a cough, "Flower-girl." I shake my head and laugh softly through the tears, holding Carl close.

I'd forgotten about the crowd, but I'm once again aware of the growing murmurs, and then a woman's shrill voice rings out, "Black magic!" When I look up, it's Abigail, Fauna's former caregiver from White Oak Manor. She's pointing at me with fierce eyes.

"*No* . . . it's *not*," I stutter. "I've been trying to—"

A crazed man interrupts me. "You witch!" he spews.

The next thing I know, another man appears with a chainsaw. "Down with the tree!" He revs it with a sinister rumble. "Down with all the trees! Bring anything you've got!"

A herd of people haphazardly take off running toward their cars and houses.

"The trees are not our enemies!" I plead as I help Carl up. But a group of men with axes and saws are already coming toward us. "You can't do this," I beg. "This is a mistake!"

The men storm right past us. "Get out of our way," one snarls. Within seconds, chainsaw man is gathering the axe wielders, surrounding the majestic white oak tree that has been providing shade for us for generations.

Remember me were its last words to me.

But it has mounted its own attack. In its defense against the mob, I witness branches reaching down and grabbing people at random. I close my eyes and my lightning marks scream with pain, as if I can physically feel the injury to the tree as the men hack and saw and grind in a frenzy to save those being tree-jacked. When I open my eyes, more men are charging toward us with cutting tools.

I turn to Carl. "What are we going to do?"

The oak is fighting, but even in its enormity, it doesn't stand a chance against the mounting number of residents assailing it.

Carl says something to me, but the pain I feel with each chop, each cut, is so intense that I can't hear him. I am spinning, sinking. And then I'm floating through the air, faces passing me like shadows in a dream, the strikes waning into a distant horror.

A SILVERY JINGLE nudges me awake. Mom rushes into the Book Nook and Chief Batista carries me inside and sets me in the armchair.

"Are you alright?" Mom asks. "Are you hurt?"

She fetches a glass of water and forces it to my lips, but I pull away.

I spot Carl behind Chief Batista, still gray but miraculously alive.

"That was incredibly brave, what you did back there," the chief says.

My eyes dart around the room. "Where's Fauna?"

"What do you mean?" Mom says. "She's at White Oak."

I shake my head. "No . . . she's with Aaron. I left her with Aaron."

Mom's eyes pierce mine. "Where?"

"In the town square." Before Mom can say anything else, I pull out my phone. "I'll call him."

But Carl has already dialed Aaron on his phone and hands it to me. The hollow ring echoes again and again. *Pick up, pick up, pick up.*

No answer.

I text him.

> Where are you? We're at the
> Book Nook. Please come
> with Fauna.
> Flora

Mom frantically calls Rhonda to see if Fauna has been returned to White Oak Manor, but she hasn't.

"We'll meet you back here," Chief Batista says, heading out the door with Carl.

"She's my daughter," Mom says. "I'm going too."

I pull myself up. "If you're going looking for Fauna, I'm coming with you." I hand Carl's phone back to him.

Chief Batista turns to me and shakes his head. "We can't all go. Someone needs to stay here in case they show up."

I shoot Carl a pleading look, hoping he'll volunteer to stay.

Mom touches his arm. "For all we know you nearly died back there. You'd better stay here."

Carl hesitates, then reluctantly concedes, rocking on his heels like he might pass out. I grab his shoulder to steady him, then Mom and I guide him to the armchair.

"You're not looking too good, Carl," Mom says. "After what you've been through, I think I'd better stay with you."

Chief Batista turns to me.

"Looks like it's just you and me, Miss Reed."

50

FAUNA

Fear.

I can feel the boy's fear in his every step.

No matter what is coming, I have this moment.

This moment of resting my head against his shoulder and letting him carry my fear.

I can hear his beating heart. His gasps of breath. His frantic footfall on the street. Him marveling: she is light as a bird.

Running.

Running.

And then he stops.

He holds me tighter.

His arms around me like the branches of a tree.

51

FLORA

"WHERE DID YOU LAST SEE THEM?" THE CHIEF ASKS
as we hasten down the street.

"In the town square . . . right before you dragged Carl up
onto the platform."

We can see a pillar of black smoke rising ominously above
the rooftops. The ache in my chest increases with each step.

Please God, please, let me find her.

When we turn the corner, I barely recognize the town
square. In the short time we've been gone, the growing mob
has lopped off a nauseating number of limbs from the oak.
There are branches all over the ground, some dragged into
burning piles. I don't see any victims still trapped, but the
shouting, the sawing, the sheer size of the crowd running
amok merges into a deafening cacophony.

Looking upon this scene, I'm filled with agony. Less
than an hour ago, I talked to the white oak. I held it in my
arms, felt it in my skin, to my core. It was a living thing, a

sentient being. It mourned its children. It let Carl go. It wanted to be remembered.

"Stop it! Stop it!" I beg, but no one hears me. I grab the branch closest to me and try to pull it from the fire. My knees sink to the ground. "It was trying to warn us," I cry. But my voice is swallowed by the chaos.

"Flora!" Chief Batista grabs my elbow and lifts me from the ground. "I need your help."

I wipe my stinging eyes and scan the appalling scene. There is no sign of Fauna or Aaron, but I spot Fauna's wheelchair in the distance, toppled over. "Look!" I say.

Chief Batista zeroes in on the abandoned wheelchair and we both rush over to it. "Where do you think they'd go?" he asks.

A faint trail of dandelions and daisies across the lawn leads to White Oak Manor. "I think I know," I say, grabbing the chief's wrist. "Come on!"

When I push open the heavy black door, no one is at the reception desk. Rhonda's computer is missing, and her desk is a mess, like someone took a swipe at everything that was on it.

"Rhonda?" My voice echoes in the entrance hall. "Hello?"

"Who's there?" A lanky security guard comes around the corner with his baton raised. "Oh, I thought you were looters." He lowers his baton and nods to Chief Batista.

"We're looking for Fauna Reed," the chief says. "Have you seen her? She's with a teenage boy named Aaron—"

"Blumenfeld," I fill in.

The guard shakes his head. "I moved everyone to the East Wing, but I don't recall seeing Fauna, or a young boy. Just the residents . . . and the looters I had to chase out."

Chief Batista frowns. "They'll go after just about anything they can get their hands on when they think the police are occupied, won't they?"

The security guard snorts, "Bastards. Stealing from the sick and elderly."

Chief Batista sighs heavily, then turns to me. "Now what, Miss Reed?"

I'm at a loss. But then a slight movement in the middle of the hallway grabs my attention: a few steps from us, a tiny, ragged blue jay is looking at me. I didn't see it fly in and my heart leaps.

"Shh," I say to Chief Batista, taking a step toward the door. The bird tips its head as I push the door open, then flies out and lands on the lamppost across the street. "Come on," I say, tugging on the chief's sleeve.

The blue jay dashes to a power line, then to the roof of the old movie theatre, then to another lamppost, like a blue arrow showing us the way.

"I don't under—" the chief begins, but a shriek cuts through his words.

"Help! Somebody! It just took her!"

I don't want to lose sight of the blue jay, but I break into a run with Chief Batista toward the voice and find a woman wrestling with a linden tree. A child is entangled in the branches, choking and turning blue, and the mother is clutching her in a futile attempt to pull her to safety.

I throw myself at the tree trunk while Chief Batista takes on the branches. *Please,* I tell it, *she's just a child.* My skin picks up a current that burns in my lightning marks, but I can't make out the words. It's like the linden tree speaks a different dialect than the oak trees, a mumbling that is foreign to me. *Please, let go of her,* I beg.

The woman emits hoarse, broken sounds. On the ground lies a pink stuffed dinosaur, its shiny button eyes staring up at me. *Let go,* I command the golden flowers, the heart-shaped leaves, the slender twigs. *Let go.*

The current that flows from the tree suddenly forms a single unmistakable syllable: *No.*

I push away from the trunk with an exasperated exhale. "I can't help! It won't listen!"

Chief Batista grasps at the coiling branches with his bare hands, catching one just before it ensnares him. He twists it until it breaks with a *snap,* then yanks hard on the last one holding the girl. It snaps too, and he throws it to the ground.

"Stand back!" Chief Batista says. He carries the girl away from the tree, lays her gently on the ground, and checks for a pulse.

The woman is shaking and sobbing and I let her cling to me, her fingernails digging into my arm, as the chief tilts back the child's head and blows into her tiny mouth. We can see her chest swell, then he places his hands over her ribs. "One-and-two-and-three-and-four-and-five-and-six." He pushes down with swift movements as he counts. "Seven-and-eight-and-nine-and-ten."

The girl is pale and still, and her forehead is marked with scratches forming an uneven, bleeding X.

"Fifteen-sixteen-seventeen..."

"Come on," I whisper. "Come back to us."

"Twenty-one-twenty-two-twenty-three..."

Come back.

"Twenty-six-twenty-seven-twenty-eight—"

The girl suddenly draws a deep breath and blinks. Chief Batista exhales hard and rests his hands on his knees.

"Annie!" the woman cries. She lifts her daughter and presses her to her chest, rocking from side to side. "Annie, Annie, Annie."

I pick up the dinosaur and brush off a yellow flower, assuming it belongs to the little girl. I hold it out to her and she reaches for it. Her small hands find the tail and pull the soft tip over her chin, a gesture she must have made a thousand times.

Chief Batista gets to his feet, taking measured breaths.

"Thank you," the woman says, squeezing his hand. "You saved my baby. How can I ever thank you enough?"

The chief nods humbly. "Just take her to a hospital as soon as possible. And I know I don't have to tell you to stay away from trees."

The woman nods and buries her face in the girl's hair. For a moment, I watch them and wish that Fauna could be like that child, safe in her mother's arms.

I turn to Chief Batista. "We have to go."

"You alright?" he asks the mother.

"Yes. I think so," she says.

He brushes off his dark pants and we return to the lamppost. But the blue jay is gone.

I spin on my heel. *Where did he go?*

In the distance, I hear chirping and turn in that direction. Squinting, I see a bundle of feathers on a road sign by the tunnel under the railroad tracks.

"Over there!" I say, running without waiting for the chief.

Here, here, here, the jay seems to call out.

When I reach the tunnel, there are voices. My footsteps echo in the tunnel as I draw near the shadows at the other end.

"Hand. Her. Over," a man says sternly.

Squinting again, I see the silhouette of Aaron, crouched over Fauna in his arms. He holds her gently, but his shoulders and the thrust of his chin dare anyone to come at him. His defiant answer stabs the air.

"You. Can't. Have. Her."

52

FAUNA

I could sense it before it happened, but I didn't know it would be like this.

I sensed darkness, not the beating heart.

I sensed violence, not the tender arms holding me.

Far away, a blue jay calling.

The salty scent of his neck. This is what I will remember. The moment of tenderness.

Before the carnage.

53

FLORA

"STAY BACK!" CHIEF BATISTA YELLS, BOLTING PAST ME.

He shoves me a bit too hard into the tunnel wall, making me fall to my knees.

"Hands over your heads!" he commands, aiming his gun at the five guys who have cornered Aaron and Fauna in the underpass.

"We didn't do anything," one kid says smugly, a gaping backpack slung over his shoulder with two gun barrels poking out. His buddy is holding a desktop computer screen, and another guy clutches a bulky box.

"Is that so?" the chief says, eyeing their loot.

I stand up and see Aaron glance my way. He's crouched against the curved wall with Fauna's head resting on his shoulder.

"Hands up. Now!" Chief Batista takes a step closer, his gun pointing to backpack guy.

The kid smirks, then nods to the rest of the group.

Computer guy puts the screen on the ground and box guy shrugs. Chief Batista flicks his gun to set the box down, then aims at each of them in a sweeping motion. They raise their hands, then the chief gestures with his head for Aaron to leave.

Aaron carefully adjusts Fauna in his arms and stands up.

"Now you kids get out of here," the chief shouts to us.

"But—" I start.

"Just go!"

As we scuttle away, I hear one of the guys say, "That's the other freak. Better watch out guys . . . both of them together could be lethal." They cackle amongst themselves as Chief Batista's voice echoes, "Calling all units, backup required in the underpass by the train station."

Once we're outside the tunnel, in the waning sunshine dimmed by smoke, Aaron squints at me. "'I'll be right back,' huh?"

I squint back with a grimace. "I'm sorry. I had no idea . . ."

He lets out a somber half laugh. "Who could have?"

"I know, but . . ." A strand of Fauna's wild hair has come loose from her braid and I tuck it behind her ear. "Just . . . thank you for taking care of her."

"No problem." He shifts Fauna's weight in his arms. "Well, actually . . . we did run into a few problems, but I was happy to help. I mean, not exactly happy, but . . ."

I nod. "I get it." I put my hand on Aaron's shoulder. "Seriously. Thank you."

His eyes show that vulnerability I've come to know, making me want to hug him. He has been running across town with Fauna pressed to his chest, and still he holds her like it's no effort at all.

"I'm guessing you didn't get my message?" I say. "About meeting us at the Book Nook."

"I've been kind of busy," he says with a crooked smile.

"Right."

We walk a few steps in silence, then I ask, "So why did you ditch the wheelchair?"

"I wouldn't have if Fauna wasn't so small. But the crowd was getting violent, and I figured I could move faster carrying her. I hope that was okay."

"You were trying to keep my sister out of danger. Anything you did to keep her safe would have been okay."

He tips his head. "We were fine really, until those thugs came after us."

I'm about to ask him what happened when a gunshot rings out behind us. Then another.

Chief Batista beelines out of the tunnel. "Go, go, go!" he commands, herding us in front of him.

"What happened?" I ask.

"Your mom's bookshop! Now!" The chief scoops Fauna from Aaron's arms and urges us on. "It's not safe out here."

We rush down Main Street toward the sound of sirens. There are trucks and firefighters everywhere. Flames are licking the white façade of the town hall, turning it black.

Thick smoke billows from the roof and windows, mixing with smoke from the white oak burn piles.

But all of the firefighters seem to be on Main Street, furiously fighting the linden trees with the townspeople. Chainsaws whir like metallic insects chewing a thousand twigs while the town hall rages like an abandoned ship sinking in a sea of flames. Behind me I can hear Chief Batista asking his officers what's happening. I turn around to see him crouch down with Fauna in his arms and press his police radio to his ear.

"You let him get away?" he yells. "He was threatening a minor!" The radio transforms the voice at the other end into a short static noise, and Chief Batista turns to the flaming building. "Yeah, I'm looking at it right now. It's Armageddon."

The smoke makes me cough and my eyes sting. Chief Batista nudges me from behind, Fauna's knees poking my back. "The Book Nook," he shouts.

I am suddenly disoriented with the air so full of swirling ash and smoke, but then I get my bearings and grab Aaron's arm. I'm pulling him with me when I stumble over something in the street. I look down and am horrified to see a woman's feet, her nails painted bright red, sticking out from under a tarp. One sandal is missing, and the other is twisted at a weird angle. She must have been crushed by one of the trees, then dropped back into the street. Some compassionate person took the time in the mayhem to cover her, but I can't help but wonder who she is. *Someone's wife. Someone's mother.*

"Flora!" Chief Batista belts. "We can't stop!"

I pick up running over trampled heart-shaped leaves and darting around scattered branches. At this end of Main Street, the smoke is thinning but I can still taste it.

I yank open the door and let the chief go in first with Fauna.

Mom jumps up. "Thank God!" She rushes up to Chief Batista and cradles Fauna's face in her hands. "There you are, my darling." She hugs Fauna tightly. "I was so worried."

Carl gets up from the armchair so Chief Batista can set Fauna in it. When the chief turns around, Mom throws her arms around him. "Thank you," she sobs.

Now that I've stopped running, I start coughing so hard that convulsions wrack my body.

"Hey, flower-girl," Carl says, stroking my back with concern. "Damn. It must be pretty bad out there."

I nod, catching my breath. "You should see the fire . . . and the trees attacking people . . . and all the cutting." I can't bring myself to mention the dead lady.

"Oh man," Carl whispers, pulling me to him. With my head on his chest, I notice that he and Mom have carried the old floral couch down the stairs and pushed it against the counter, which is crowded with water bottles, paper towels, and a hammer and nails. On the floor there's a pile of wooden boards wrenched from shipping crates.

"Does this mean you're feeling better?" I ask, pulling myself back at arm's length. "I mean . . . I see you've been redecorating." I nod to the couch and erupt in coughs again.

"Just a precaution." He hands me a water bottle. "Here, drink this."

The water is cool against my throat and seems to wash away the smoke. Mom is kneeling next to Fauna, giving her water too.

"We were just about to fix the hole in the door and cover up the shop windows," Carl says. "With you here now," he says to Aaron, "I won't need Mrs. Reed's help."

Carl grabs the hammer and a handful of nails. "You okay, now?" he asks me.

"I think so."

Aaron's about to lift a board when Chief Batista's radio crackles. He heads to the end of one of the aisles. I'm wondering how he can stay here with everything going on when Carl nods toward him and pulls me onto the couch. Aaron sinks down next to us. Mom is murmuring sweetly to Fauna in the corner as the three of us lean in, trying to overhear the chief's conversation. Static obscures some of the words, but I can make out Officer Herrera's voice, saying people are looking for us. Chief Batista responds, "I have both the girls here. I'll make sure they're protected."

Protected. No wonder the chief is still here, I realize. *We're a target. People are out to get us.*

Images of the guys in the tunnel and Chief Batista

shouting "Go, go, go" flash before my eyes. I look at Fauna in the armchair, at her pale face and thin body. How could anyone see her as a threat?

The chief is coming back toward us when there's a sudden *bang*. Thick branches of a linden tree thrash against the shop window, as if it's reaching for us. I cling to Carl as chainsaws rev and men shout, then feel the waning current in my lightning marks as the branches fall away.

Aaron lowers his water bottle and looks at me. "This is insane," he says. "There are crazy people out there who actually think you did all this. You and . . ." He nods to Fauna.

"But we didn't! How can they think—"

Carl puts his hand on my shoulder. "*We* know that."

"There are all kinds of rumors going around, though," Aaron says ". . . things about you being witches and stuff."

I grit my teeth. *People can be such jerks.*

Aaron types into his phone. "Oh, man. Check this out."

On the screen is a video of the white oak grabbing Carl. There's no sound, only the branches lifting him like a puppet, playing over and over and over. The caption reads: NOT A HOAX: TEEN ATTACKED BY TREE.

Aaron studies his phone. "It's going viral. Like, literally, right now."

"Who uploaded it?" Carl asks.

"I don't know. It's just a random username."

As the guys inspect the video, Chief Batista taps on his phone and brings it to his ear. I try not to look like I'm eavesdropping as he distances himself down the aisle again.

"Where are your guys?" A pause. "No, no, this is way beyond Chester now." . . . "I was there, I saw it with my own eyes. We need state, federal, National Guard, military, whatever we can get." He sighs. "Okay, let me know."

He pulls his hand across his face, then makes another call. "Mayor, yes . . . What the hell?" . . . "What do you mean your hands are tied?" He paces back and forth. "You need to issue a city-wide, twenty-four-hour shelter-in-place mandate. I don't want to see any civilians on the streets until we have the situation under control." . . . "I'm telling you, it's not safe. There are looters and all kinds of people out there." . . . "Of course I called for backup," he barks. "They should be here within the hour." The chief nods with exasperation. "Fine. You do that."

He hangs up and turns to me.

"Miss Reed." He motions me over, then he guides me to the back of the shop. "I need you to tell me everything."

I TAKE IN a breath and tell the chief how it started with the lightning strike and Fauna falling out of the oak tree. I tell him about my father, my connection to the oak, the Lichtenberg figures on my arms and neck. I tell him about the blue jay and the acorns. I show him the pictures I took in Dad's old shed and the logo with the cracked seed that Carl and I saw in the YouTube video.

"May I?" he asks. He takes my phone and sends himself the photos. When he's finished, he says, "Go on."

I fill in all the details I can think of, and as I do, I can't help but feel relief to put it all into words, to be listened to. The chief has seen for himself what's happening, and I can tell he no longer sees me as delusional.

Carl comes up to us. "Hey, not to interrupt. But I thought you'd want to know, Chief." He reads from his phone: "Breaking news, developing story . . . Derwyn, Pennsylvania . . . fires, riots, looting and mysterious deaths, bodies found in trees, unclear what is the cause."

"So the news is getting out," the chief says. He rubs his forehead and checks his watch. "Where is that backup?" He walks to the front of the store. Carl and Aaron have boarded the bottom half of the hole in the door, and Chief Batista peers out the gap above it. He immediately pulls back.

"Get down!" he orders. "Flora, Mrs. Reed . . ."

Mom and I dash behind a bookshelf and Chief Batista rushes to Fauna. He lifts her from the armchair and carries her to me, laying her gently in my lap. "We've got company," he says.

A man shouts from the street. "We're here to talk with Flora and Fauna Reed." I recognize Mr. Dunne's voice. "And Carl Nielsen."

Aaron and Carl are already pushing the couch across the floor to block the entrance.

"We just want to talk," Mr. Dunne, barks. "Nicely."

I peer through the space between the books and the shelf, where I can see through the shop's front display window. A group of men is gathered outside the shop.

"No can do," the chief shouts, kneeling on the couch with his gun pointed out the gap.

A murmur rises from the street. I don't think the mob expected Chief Batista to be here, and he has his pistol aimed right at Mr. Dunne. I hold my breath in the silence as Mr. Dunne scans the men behind him. He nods and I expect them all to walk away, but Mr. Dunne faces the shop again.

"Either you send Carl and the girls out, or we come in."

54

FAUNA

Fire.

Deep tremors in the earth, a warning from all directions.

"...Fire...Fire."

Seedlings crouching, saplings weeping, trees trembling.

"Mother Tree, where are you?"

Silence.

55

FLORA

I KEEP MY EYES ON CHIEF BATISTA.

"Come on, Mike, they're just kids," he shouts.

"SO WAS MY BOY," Mr. Dunne shouts back.

Chief Batista holds his gun steady. "I'm sorry about your son. But this"—he flicks the pistol back and forth—"it won't solve anything."

A man yells, "They're behind it all, and you know it!"

"Go home, all of you!" Chief Batista urges. "No one's allowed on the streets right now." Carl starts to get up from where he's squatting near the door and the chief flinches. *Stay down*, his glance says.

"Not until you give us the boy and the tree talker and her little witch sister," Mr. Dunne persists.

I hug Fauna tighter, her soft ginger hair against my chin.

"The law still applies, Dunne! Crimes will be punished. Criminals will be brought to justice—"

"Spare me your law-and-order talk! Just send them out!" He pauses. "NOW."

I can sense that Chief Batista is done shouting through the crack in the door, and that he's done negotiating. "There's nothing for you here, Mike. The kids are in a safe location with the police."

Mr. Dunne lets out a booming laugh. "How stupid do you think I am? I DIDN'T COME HERE TO PLAY HIDE-AND-SEEK. WE KNOW THEY'RE IN THERE."

The chief shakes his head. "We're finished here, Dunne. Go home!" He gets on his feet and moves away from the door, just as Carl crawls past me, putting a finger to his lips.

Mom suddenly gets up and leans toward the gap in the door. "He's right! They're not here!"

Her hands are trembling but her voice is strong.

"And there's another little witch," someone hollers.

The mob laughs.

"Burn the witch," Mr. Dunne yells. "Burn the whole place down!"

Chief Batista motions for Mom to return to where I'm hiding with Fauna and moves back to the door. "Alright. That's enough! We'll have none of that talk. I'm not going to tell you again to go home!" He moves his gun in a sweeping motion. "I *will* shoot anyone who approaches this building or dares to threaten Mrs. Reed or these kids!"

My heart is racing as Carl nudges me.

"We can go out the back," he whispers. "It's clear."

He tells Mom to go and takes Fauna from me, staying as low as he can. "Go," he says.

Just then, Chief Batista bellows, "Hey!" In a flash, I look up to see a man's arm raised. The chief fires a shot. Then the front window shatters into a torrent of glass and fire.

I bend over Fauna and see broken bottles roll across the floor: Molotov cocktails. Mom's life's work—the shelves full of stories and the memories of afternoons with Fauna after school—erupt into flames before my eyes.

"To the back! To the back!" Chief Batista shouts. Carl shields Fauna and me with his broad shoulders as we stumble through the smoke and out the back door. Aaron and Chief Batista scramble out behind us.

"Stay together and get yourselves home!" the chief urges. "I need to make sure the backup has arrived, then I'll meet you there!" He is already running toward the town square when he adds, "Prepare to leave town!"

The five of us take off down the backstreet behind the shops. We are close to the corner when we hear footsteps and voices. Carl dashes behind a dumpster and I pull Mom around it with me. Aaron follows just in time as three guys with guns pass us.

When the coast is clear, Carl hands Fauna to Aaron and darts out. He climbs into an old truck at one of the loading docks and waves us toward him. "Come on!"

Mom and I clamber into the pickup's frayed back seat and Aaron holds up Fauna so we can secure her across our laps. Then he slams the door shut and hops into the front seat next to Carl. I hold Fauna's head against my chest. The engine is already running.

"Hold on," Carl says. He tugs at the gear shift and hits the gas pedal, then turns into the narrow backstreet. Picking up speed, Carl chants "Move, move, move" as we close in on the mob coming up the street.

"Out of the way!" Aaron yells out the window. Backpack guy from the tunnel looks up and swiftly grabs a gun from over his shoulder.

"Get down!" I shout. I bend over Fauna just as a bullet ricochets off the hood of the truck. Carl swerves and we scrape against a brick wall. I keep my head down with my body crouched over Fauna.

"Watch out!" Aaron says. I look up and see him pointing at an abandoned blue van in the middle of the road. Carl jerks the wheel and the tires screech. I hold tight to Fauna. "Oh, my God," Mom mutters. I turn to see the van's windows smashed in and its side scratched as if marked by claws.

We fly down the road and Carl seems to be in control until we see a huge maple stretching its limbs over the street just ahead. Carl pumps the brakes. As if in slow motion, my eyes are drawn to a body entangled in the branches, its neon orange running shoes glowing against the foliage. Next to it, another branch is wriggling and coiling, reaching toward us.

"Go faster!" I implore Carl. "Faster!"

He pounds the accelerator, then squeals around a corner

and onto a main road. Suddenly, it's strangely bright. In an instant I realize why.

There are no trees blocking the sky. Stumps are all that remain lining the sidewalk, with branches piled high along the curb.

"Hang on," Carl says. The truck bounces wildly over remnants of cuttings halfway down Maple Street. Mom and I clutch Fauna tightly. *Only a little bit farther*, I think. And then we all see it. A massive tree has been felled and its trunk is blocking most of the road. Some of its branches are pointed right at us. Carl's foot lands hard on the brakes, but it's not soon enough. The truck skids and Aaron throws himself against the door in the nick of time as limbs crash through the windshield. I hear Carl wail as Aaron takes quick, shallow breaths, a branch only inches from his face.

I can't see Carl, but Aaron jumps out and swings the back door open. "Give me Fauna! I'll follow you to your house."

Mom and I slide out the passenger side. "Carl!" I call out. I hear him wail again, then jump out the driver door. When he reaches me, there's fresh blood on his shirt. His arm is hanging limp by his side and he's grasping it, opening and closing his hand to test his mobility.

"You're hurt!" I say, touching his chest.

"I'll be okay. We have to go!"

We take off running but Carl is still holding his arm, slowing him down. I keep my pace even with his, glancing his way every other step. Seeing his bloody shirt sends an internal lightning bolt through my heart. Carl seems to shake off everything, like there's nothing he hasn't already been through. But I can see that he's wincing and am afraid of how hurt he might be.

Aaron and Mom are ten steps ahead of us as we near the hawthorn hedge. I suddenly realize that there might be more men waiting at our house for us and picture rifles pointed in our direction when we arrive. But just as I'm wondering what we'll do if that happens, Mom and Aaron both stop cold. Mom raises her hand to her mouth, like she's stifling a scream, as Carl and I see it too.

It's Mrs. Walsh. She's entangled in her roses, pressed against the brick wall of her cottage, high up under the eaves. She isn't moving. Her face is twisted and her mouth is open. Her eyes stare straight at us and the mark on her forehead leaves no room for doubt.

"It's not only the trees . . ." Mom whispers. "It's more than that . . . just like David said."

56

FAUNA

Loss.

Trees feel it too.

A Mother Tree that is cut down and burned, black smoke trailing into the sky.

Friends that are axed down, one by one, falling into each other's arms.

A sister forest that is burning, sending messages of warning.

A planet that cries out in agony.

And then nothing.

A void.

The ultimate loss.

57

FLORA

WHEN WE REACH THE HAWTHORN HEDGE, MY
lightning marks start tingling in the strange new language
I'm only starting to understand. I'm still reeling over what
happened to Mrs. Walsh, but I'm relieved not to see a band
of townspeople on our lawn as we rush up the driveway.

Mom's trembling hands fumble with the key as she tries
to unlock the front door.

"Hurry, Mom," I plead, scanning the yard. "They could
have followed us!"

"I'm trying," she pants.

When the door flings open, we all tumble in and Mom
slams it behind us. We stand staring at each other, our chests
heaving, as if we have a dozen questions but no words to ar-
ticulate them.

Finally, Mom says, "I'll get us some water."

Aaron lays Fauna gently on the sofa.

"I'll get the first-aid kit," I tell Carl. I go into the kitchen
to retrieve it from the pantry and see Mom holding on to

the sink in the dim evening light, the sun's last rays seeming to reach for her in comfort.

"Is Carl okay?" she asks, wiping her face quickly.

"I hope so," I say. "Are you?"

She nods but it's more of a shrug. She's always so strong, but I know none of us can really say we're alright. The world is turning upside-down and no one knows how to stop it. *Except maybe Dad*, I think. I wonder if Mom's thinking the same but I don't dare ask.

I grab the tin box filled with medical supplies. "I'm going to bandage Carl's arm up," I tell her.

She nods again and pulls glasses from the cabinet.

Carl is already in the guest bathroom, bent over the sink and sloshing water onto his arm. I cringe when I see his wound. It's the size of a nickel, and the white porcelain sink is striped red with his blood.

"*Crap*," I say.

He swallows hard. "Exactly."

I pry open the box and rummage through it. *Antiseptic. Gauze. Paper tape.* I look up and see blood still pouring from his arm. "I don't know if this will be enough."

He winces. "Just . . . give me that wad of gauze to hold on it. Maybe I can stop the bleeding."

I pass it to him and he winces again as he presses.

I grimace as if his pain is mine. "What happened to you back there?"

"A branch . . . when we crashed. It punctured my arm."

I frown again. "Oh man. And then you what? Just yanked it out?"

"What else could I do? I had to."

My heart aches thinking about how painful that must have been for him. We stand there in silence for a few moments. "And the truck?" I ask tentatively, lowering my voice. "How did you know how to start it?"

"Oh that." He gives me a crooked smile. "Those old cars are easy-peasy."

The gauze has turned red and I fold up another thick wad and hand it to him. I'm about to comment on his car-stealing ability when he looks at me affectionately.

"I'm sorry," he says. "For everything you've been through these past few days."

I look away, then back at Carl. "You've been through a lot too." *And not just in the last few days,* I want to say.

He shrugs.

I peer up at him and bite my lip. "I know it'll hurt, but I'm going to need to put some antiseptic on that."

He takes a deep breath and peels the gauze away. The heavy bleeding has subsided, but I can see the jagged edge of the wound.

"How do we know there aren't any wood splinters in it?" I ask him.

"It bled pretty hard. And I rinsed it pretty well before you came in, even though it hurt like hell."

I cringe inside. "I bet." I let out a little puff of air. "Okay then." I squeeze some antiseptic onto a cotton ball and dab at the wound carefully, blowing on it as he tightens his grip on the sink. Then I pull a dressing pad from its package. I gently place it over the gash and wrap gauze around it multiple times.

"You okay?" I ask.

"Yeah." Carl scratches his closely cropped curls. Then he holds the bandage tight so I can tear off pieces of paper tape. My fingers brush against his as I secure it.

"There," I say, "at least for now."

I lay my hand on his forearm and he covers it with his.

"Thank you for saving me," he says. "From the oak tree."

"Of course," I whisper. I meet his tender gaze and time seems to slow down.

He traces the pink zigzags that reach across the back of my hand. "How did you do it?" he asks. "Talk to the tree, I mean. How does it work?"

His caress makes me shiver and there is that faint whisper again through my lightning marks. *I wish I could tell her everything.*

"I don't know exactly." I take a deep breath. "It's like we speak through our skins. Through electrical currents, maybe."

Carl wraps my hand in both of his and leans closer to me. "Flora, if things go south here, will you trust me?"

I'm about to ask him what he means, but then I sense the current from his skin again. *I wish I could tell her.*

His hands cling tighter to mine.

She deserves to know about her father.

My mind races. *My father? What does Carl know about him?*

"Just say you'll trust me." His eyes are begging me.

I nod. "Okay. I'll trust you."

There's a light rap on the door. "Hey, guys," Aaron says. "Someone's here."

Carl straightens up and lets go of my hands. "Do you know who it is?"

"I'm hoping it's the chief, but I can't tell for sure."

We hurry to the living room. Mom is already at the door, and Chief Batista is dismounting his motorcycle.

"The roads are a mess," he says. "Where can I hide this?"

Mom points to our garage, which besides our old Volvo is full of boxes and Dad's stuff and rickety furniture and broken toys Mom can't bring herself to get rid of. "I'll go open the garage door," she says.

"Nice battle wound," Aaron says to Carl, elbowing him lightly. "And nice driving."

Carl punches Aaron's arm. "You survived, didn't you?"

"Barely." Aaron darts to his right, like he did in the truck to miss the branch. "Only because of my stellar reflexes."

Carl mirrors a snake move with his head and neck, then groans and brings his hand to the bandage. "Careful," I say, then laugh with them both. It feels good for a moment to be playful with them, to forget about the nightmare going on outside.

But as soon as Chief Batista comes into the house, the mood instantly grows somber again.

"Mrs. Reed," he says, "we need to discuss the plan. And quick."

Mom shifts her weight uneasily. "I thought we were going to leave town."

"I'm afraid that's not an option. The roads are too bad."

"Okay," Mom says, but it sounds like a question.

"I doubt those hooligans who are after the kids are going to try to come here tonight. But in case they do . . ." He takes a breath. "We need to keep the house dark . . . make it look like no one's here. I would've preferred to bring you to the precinct and set you up there, but like I said, the roads are too bad right now. So I think your basement is probably the best option you have."

"For how long?" Mom asks.

"I honestly don't know. I'm guessing until we can get all the trees cut down and clear the roads."

"But what about reinforcements?" I ask. "Shouldn't they be here by now?"

Chief Batista shakes his head. "I'm sorry but . . . there are no reinforcements I can call on. We're on our own."

"No reinforcements?" Carl says. "What if the mob does come here? You saw what they did to the bookshop."

"Look," Chief Batista says, "in an ideal world, I'd have a whole hoard of officers here to keep you safe. But we're not living in an ideal world right now. These tree-jackings are happening all across the state. Maybe the country even."

Mom is quiet, and it's as if I can hear her thinking.

"So it's just you," she says.

"I'm afraid so," he says humbly. "But I brought extra ammunition. And my hope is that if I'm here keeping vigilant, and someone does try to mess with you, they won't be expecting me and a few shots will scare them off." He pauses. "I know it's not a foolproof plan, but it's the best I've got under the circumstances . . . and frankly, I feel better knowing I'm the one looking after you after everything that's happened."

Mom squeezes Chief Batista's arm. "I appreciate that." She takes a big breath. "Okay, then," she says, "the basement it is." Her tone abruptly shifts into someone taking complete charge of the operation.

"Flora, you gather all the pillows and blankets you can. Carl, I don't want you carrying anything heavy with that injured arm. You can help me with your good hand . . . loading some food and bottled water into bags. Aaron, you can help us with that and carry things to the basement—just be careful on the stairs. After we get all the supplies down there, we can carry Fauna down and get ourselves situated for the night."

"And I'll keep an eye outside," the chief says.

We all disperse in silence, as if militarized for precision. I run upstairs and grab the big laundry basket. Then I start pulling pillows and blankets from the beds. I assume we'll be able to sneak upstairs to use the bathroom and do basic hygiene stuff, but I grab some towels anyway. I spot the charging station in the hallway and grab that too. I shuttle things down in multiple trips, then stop in the hall again to catch my breath.

The sun has set completely by this point. Standing there, in the glimmer of moonlight, it hits me hard that this is real. Nature rising up against us, the town hall burning, the white oak cut down and scattered all over the town square, the mob burning down the Book Nook. I inhale and exhale slowly, wishing I could stop time. Darkness would settle in its familiar corners, the buzzing cicadas and crying night birds would echo in the silent rooms, and nothing would ever change. *Change.* It took Dad away, pushed Fauna out of the oak tree, turned nature against us, killed people— *is* killing people.

"Oh my God," I say out loud. "People are dying out there."

Carl's arms are suddenly around me, like he's holding me together, his chin against my ear. My skin starts to tingle again, but I push it away, push all my questions away. I just want him to hold me.

"You can do this, flower-girl," he whispers, his breath hot against my cheek. "We'll be alright."

As I press his arms against me, his strong arms that make me feel safe, I suddenly remember his injury. "The first-aid kit," I say. "It's still in the bathroom." I start to pull away when Carl says, "Wait."

I catch lights flickering by the hawthorn hedge like fire-flies.

But within seconds, I realize they're not fireflies. At the end of our driveway, moving as if held by marauders in a medieval march, is a dancing mass of torches.

58

FAUNA

Letting go.

That is the hardest part.

An acorn, holding on to the twig.

A girl, clinging to the branch.

A tree, trembling with each strike.

There is always a moment of lingering, of floating in the air, a moment between inhales and exhales, the universe holding its breath.

Then comes the gust of wind, the flash of lightning, the blow of the axe, the exhale.

And the inevitable, irreversible, plummeting to the ground.

59

FLORA

THERE'S A FAINT CREAK FROM THE BACK DOOR AND Chief Batista's silhouette appears in the dark. "Not a sound," he whispers.

Mom eases down next to Fauna and pulls her head onto her lap. The rest of us huddle on the floor beside them as voices drift in from outside.

"No signs of the tree hugger."

"The tree *talker*, you mean."

"Whatever." A hoarse chuckle.

The voices get closer.

"When she shows up, she and her tree hugger friends"—more laughter—"they'll be marked alright."

"Yeah . . . with a bullet."

More chuckling. I barely dare to breathe. The leaping flames seem innumerable. Fifty? A hundred?

"This isn't good." Chief Batista sucks in air through his teeth. "There's too many. If they attack us, we don't stand a chance."

I sense Fauna looking at me and turn to face her. Her pale blue eyes, even in the dark, seem to tell me she wants to say something. I put my hand on her forehead. It's clammy and her hair is moist by her temples. My lightning marks pick up her fear.

Suddenly, an engine sputters, then becomes a loud whirring, punctuated by a series of revs. I stay low and rush to the window, but I can't discern more than flickering lights and shadows. That sound, though. There's no doubt. They're cutting down the oak.

Fauna screams out in pain as the chainsaw touches the tree and begins grinding through its trunk.

Grinding through my sister.

Fauna inhales sharply and arches upward, her eyes fixed toward the ceiling.

"Nooooo," I shout.

Chief Batista wraps his hand over my mouth and pulls me back. I struggle to get out of his grip, but he holds me down. "Keep quiet," he whispers brusquely.

He doesn't understand that I can feel Fauna's pain, every cut of metal teeth biting into her bones. I can't bear being restrained, having my voice silenced. *I have to help her.* I start squirming again but then stop abruptly when a thought lands hard in my mind.

Did Fauna know this would happen? Did she see it coming?

The last time she spoke to me, when we were under the oak tree, she said: *Now my destiny is fulfilled. I love you, Flora, remember that, and tell Mom I love her.* It was her final goodbye, but I didn't want to listen.

Tears spill down my face. The chief gently pulls me away from the window and Mom is cradling Fauna in her lap, probably thinking she's having another seizure.

I pry the chief's hand from my mouth. "Mom, she'll die!" My words tear a hole through the darkness. "If they cut down the tree, Fauna will die."

Chief Batista releases me and pulls out his gun. Carl rushes to his backpack and returns with a pistol. "Do you see them?" he asks the chief, crawling up next to him.

"Hold on to your sister," Mom says to me sternly. "Don't let her go."

I slide under Fauna and press her to my chest, squeeze my fingers into her cramping hands as she convulses and wails rise from her thin body. She grabs my fingers so tightly I fear she might crush them.

Mom rushes upstairs. I hear Carl fumbling with his phone and then, "It's me . . . stand by . . . possible Code Black Hawk." The sound of an armchair being dragged, breaking glass. I turn and see Chief Batista at the front window, shards gleaming from the floor, his knee propped on the chair with its back as his shield. Mom's brisk footsteps on the stairs. A gleaming rifle in her hands.

A shot echoes. Chief Batista shifts his weight to his other knee and fires two more. The whirring wanes and stops. The crowd erupts into shouts. I feel Fauna relax in my arms as Carl joins the chief with his gun poised out the broken window. I have no time to think about why Carl has a gun, who he called using code words, or why Mom has a rifle. She loads it with a *click-click*, as if she's done it before, and hurries to the front door. "Everyone quiet," she whispers loudly.

The chainsaw whirs again.

Mom throws the door open. "Oh no, you don't!"

Chief Batista darts out after her. Fauna's hands cling to mine again as she bends backward against my chest. Gunshots ring outside. A bullet hits the bookcase behind me and I duck to cover Fauna.

"Code Black Hawk!" Carl screams into his phone. "Code Black Hawk. ASAP!"

Another shot. Another. I hear Chief Batista and Mom outside, their voices ripped apart by the blasts of bullets. "Get down!" Carl shouts to Aaron and me.

Batista stumbles inside, dragging Mom. "What were you thinking?"

"They're killing my baby! We have to stop them!"

More bullets hit the walls around us. Carl is at the window beside Batista, both firing off rounds. Carl flinches as a bullet hits the window frame. My lightning marks are on fire as the jagged saw eats its way into my sister. Her back is arched, her whole body strained and twitching. I clutch her tighter and realize she's no longer breathing. "Breathe!" I beg. "Breathe!" And then suddenly, everything goes quiet.

Fauna sinks into my lap with a sharp, labored breath.

The whirring has ceased and the mob has stopped shooting back. The burning in my lightning marks subsides to a dull throbbing.

Nobody moves.

"What happened?" I ask in a low voice.

Carl whispers back. "I guess we showed them."

"Wait," Aaron says. "What was that spark? Did you see it?"

"What kind of spark?" The chief's tone is grave.

"A blue flare, like they hit something, like they cut into metal . . ." Aaron's voice trails off, then he jumps up. "Oh, man! Guys, they're going to—"

He's interrupted by a surge in the air, then a flash of light. The unmistakable crackling of flames eating wood.

The burning in my lightning marks flares as Fauna's hands squeeze my fingers again, the back of her head pressing harder and harder against my neck.

"Nooooooo!" I wail.

Fauna twists and her eyes find mine. "Remember me," her thin voice says. A tear trickles down her temple. She gasps and struggles to breathe as the pain from the fire consumes her. And then one long exhale escapes from her, and I feel the life drain out of her.

My Fauna.

My little sister.

My butterfly.

60

FAUNA

Remember me.
Please, remember me.

61

FLORA

FAUNA'S FINGERS FALL AWAY FROM MINE, AND HER delicate arm slides over the edge of the sofa, her hand opening like a flower. Her whole body goes limp in my lap, and my heart cracks apart. I immediately sense the loss, the loneliness in my lightning marks, the silence in my skin, my bones.

My little sister was just here, and now she is gone.

"My baby," Mom howls. She drags Fauna from me and pulls her to her chest, rocking as if she could bring her daughter back. "My baby," she sobs, "my baby, my baby."

I bury my face in my hands and feel Carl's arm around my shoulder. "I've got you," he says tenderly.

But I don't want Carl right now. I want my sister back. "They killed her," I scream. I slip from under Carl's arm and rush to Chief Batista. "Do something! Help her!"

Chief Batista's eyes are fixed on the burning oak, a twisted black shape in the flames, scarlet fingers reaching for the sky. I shake his shoulder. "*Help* her!"

But the chief's attention is zeroed in on the tree. I can see the flames reflected in his eyes as a loud creaking cuts through the night. The next thing I know, he pulls me away from the window. "Take cover!"

We crouch to the floor. Mom is weeping too hard to move. "Mrs. Reed!" I hear Carl shout. The whole house begins to tremble. Glass shatters as a huge flaming branch crashes into the living room and ignites the curtains. Smoke starts filling the room. From outside, I hear people cheering. *Cheering.* And Mr. Dunne's hoarse laughter rises above them all. "Burn in hell, witches!"

"We have to get out of here!" the chief commands.

Carl is suddenly beside me, his arm around my waist. Through the smoke I see Aaron grab the blanket draped over the back of the couch and wrap it around Fauna, then lift her from Mom's arms. We all dash toward the back porch, our farmhouse whining and moaning like a living thing.

"Hurry, hurry." Chief Batista throws open the door and we scramble out into the meadow. I can feel the grass wailing as we run through it—the flowers, the weeds, the withering stems, and even the stoic pillars and crowns in the forest beyond, all bracing themselves, whispering their farewells.

Once we're far enough away from the house, I come to an abrupt halt, wondering which way to run. I turn to see our home collapsing like a tower of cards. The meadow, the forest. Soon it will all be on fire.

I spin around and find Carl. "Wait," he shouts. "Everyone stop."

A thrum approaches overhead until it's so loud I have to cover my ears. I look up and see a helicopter, hovering like a giant insect. The wind from the rotor blades forces me downward. As if from a lifetime ago, I remember Fauna's voice calling my name as she searched for me in the tall grass.

Carl pulls me up, but I resist. "Come on," he yells, dragging me toward the flattening patch around the helicopter as it touches down.

"Who are they?" I scream.

But Carl only pulls me more forcefully.

Squinting into the gusts of searing wind, I see the door open and a man step out. His hair sways wildly in the downwash. "Get on board!" he shouts, waving us toward him.

Mom hesitates, then gasps. "David?"

The fire casts light on his face and I recognize him too.

Dad.

He ushers Mom and me first, then the boys. Chief Batista hops in just before Dad closes the door behind us and shouts to the cockpit, "All set!"

We scurry into short rows of seats that face each other and get strapped in. Carl, me, the chief. Aaron, Mom, Dad. The only illumination comes from the glow of the cockpit controls and a few muted lights along the seams. I can see Mom holding Fauna in her lap, wrapped like a sleeping baby.

There's a surge in my stomach as the helicopter lifts from the ground. As we rise into the night sky, Chief Batista humbly introduces himself to Dad.

"David Reed," Dad says in reply.

David Reed.

The man I've missed all these years, the one I reached out to on the off chance he would answer me, the one I hoped would help me bring Fauna out of her catatonic state. He's right here in front of me, in the dim light, like a mirage.

"Thanks for this." Chief Batista motions to the inside of the helicopter. "Where are you taking us?"

Dad leans in. "A secure location." He taps the emblem on the wall behind him, lit just enough for me to see it: a diamond-shaped logo with a seed cracked open. *The logo from the video.*

Dad leans forward and squeezes my knee. "My Flora," he says, lingering on me. Then he leans diagonally across the aisle and clasps Carl's hand. "We came as fast as we could."

Carl nods, and then Dad settles back in his seat next to Mom and asks, "What's wrong with Fauna?"

I gaze into my lap. It's loud in the helicopter, but even if the words are muffled, I can't bear witnessing Mom tell Dad that Fauna is gone. I abruptly shift my thoughts to why Dad just shook Carl's hand and spoke to him as if they knew each other, *have* known each other, maybe for a long time.

Carl must read my mind because I feel him touch my arm, but I pull away. The boy next door, *my* boy next door, the kiss, everything. Was it just pretend? He knew where my dad was all along? Carl takes my hand, squeezes my fingers, and I remember his words: *Will you follow me? Promise to trust me no matter what?* And the faint current that whispered to me earlier: *I wish I could tell her everything.*

I untangle my fingers from his and turn to face him. "So you know my dad? He sent you?"

Carl leans in close. "To keep you safe. To protect you."

I look over and see Mom's face buried in Fauna's hair, Dad's head in his hands.

The helicopter sways and below us I can see the remains of our house charring, the fallen oak tree in flames, the fires dotting the landscape all the way to the town square, burning like a war zone. My hometown, our farmhouse, our street, The Wee Reed Book Nook, the town hall, White Oak Manor. All gone. My beloved little sister, swaddled in Mom's arms, looking as if she's merely resting.

I close my eyes and feel the stinging of tears. Fragmented thoughts and half-formed prayers tumble around my head, begging to be woken up from this nightmare to a summer morning, to birds chirping by my window, to the sun peeking through the curtains, to Fauna's laughter in the kitchen and the smell of Mom's pancakes.

I open my eyes and shift in my seatbelt. It's pressing on something in the pocket of my jeans, and I lean back and pull it out.

The acorn Fauna gave me under the oak tree.

Remember the acorns, she told me. *They fall off the tree and into the soil where they sprout into new beings, new trees. It will be like that, like a rebirth.*

I hold it tightly and let the tears come. Above us the stars are burning like fires and below us the fires are burning like stars and I feel like we are floating, rocking, between two shadowy worlds.

Like a rebirth.

Carl takes my hand again and I let him.

This day has been interminable, this night surreal. We have lost nearly everything and I have no idea where we'll go from here, what nature will do to humanity. The thumping of the rotor blades above me beats in tandem with my aching heart, reminding me the world as I know it will never be the same.

I cling to the acorn, my last gift from Fauna, then caress the smooth surface, like I'm hoping to find a door, like I could crawl up inside and be born again in a shady forest next to my sister.

I suddenly detect something I hadn't felt before. It's too dark to see, but I run my nail over the spot and am certain it's a crack. *An opening for a sprout.*

The familiar tingling travels up my arm as Fauna's last words to me under the lightning tree are whispered in my mind.

We will meet again.

62

FAUNA

Like butterflies, fluttering in the meadow.
Like sparks, glowing in the night.
Like a seed, cracking open.
Upward, upward.
Into the sky.

ABOUT THE AUTHOR

LENE FOGELBERG is the *Wall Street Journal* bestselling author of *Beautiful Affliction: A Memoir*. She loves to explore the world and has lived all over the globe—in a small Pennsylvania town, as well as in Germany, Malaysia, and Indonesia. She currently resides in her native Sweden with her family. *The Lightning Tree* is the first book in her YA trilogy, The Natural Intelligence Revolution. You can learn more about Lene's books online at www.lenefogelberg.com.